GW00836007

D1

# Gently Mistaken

## Also by Alan Hunter

# GENTLY MISTAKEN

## Alan Hunter

Constable · London

First published in Great Britain 1999
by Constable & Company Limited
3 The Lanchesters, 162 Fulham Palace Road
London W6 9ER
Copyright © Alan Hunter 1999
The right of Alan Hunter to be
identified as the author of this work
has been asserted by him in accordance
with the Copyright, Designs and Patents Act 1988
ISBN 0 094 79430 8
Set in Palatino by
SetSystems Ltd, Saffron Walden, Essex
Printed and bound in Great Britain
by MPG Books Ltd, Bodmin, Cornwall

A CIP catalogue record for this book
is available from the British Library

# 1

'It's that Ford woman on the phone, sir. Says she may have something for you.'

Gently frowned and looked up from the report he was checking through. 'Did she say what?'

'No sir. Just that she thought you ought to know. But if you like I'll tell her you're busy, sir, and get her to leave it with me.'

Gently shrugged and stared out of the window at the landscape of roofs and distant cranes. It was August and the city was bathed in misty sunlight. Traffic was light in the street below and even crime seemed to have taken a holiday. Since the Hastings case, a fortnight earlier, little fresh had landed on his desk.

He picked up the phone. 'Put her through, then.'

He toyed with the pipe that lay in his ashtray. A moment later he heard the voice of Oswald Hastings' secretary, sounding as though it were coming from a distance.

'Is that you, sir?'

'Gently speaking.'

'I don't know . . . but I thought I should tell you. I'm up at Shinglebourne for the Festival and yesterday, I'm almost certain . . .'

'You are in Shinglebourne?'

'Yes . . . do you know it?'

Gently sighed. Yes, he knew Shinglebourne. The small town stretched by a pebbly beach where, each year, was held the celebrated Festival. There lived his friends, the Capels, and there, twice before, he had been called out on business. But what had Shinglebourne to do with a case that centred on Fulham and Putney?

'So what have you to tell me?'

'Well, yesterday evening ... would you know the road up the coast to Holmeness?'

'I know it.'

'Yes. Well, my friend and I thought we'd take an evening drive to Holmeness. There was only a recital on at the church and neither of us wanted to go to it ...'

'Does this have to do with the case?'

'Yes, but I need to tell you – '

She sounded nervous. Christine Ford. A well-equipped blonde of around thirty.

'If you remember that road ... but perhaps you don't? It leaves the town quite abruptly. Then there's nothing till you come to Holmeness, another two miles up the coast. That is, there's nothing except an old railway coach that must have been dumped there when they closed the line. It stands about two hundred yards up the road, with brambles and things growing round it – quite dilapidated. And it was there, as we were driving past ...'

'Yes?'

'I – well ... A man was sitting outside it.'

'A man ...?'

'Yes, I'm sorry. And I'm almost certain it was him.'

'Was ...?'

'Do I have to tell you? I think it was Jason sitting there.'

'Jason ... Thorpe.'

'Yes – Jason. Who you've been looking for all this time.'

There were noises at the other end of the phone.

'I can't swear to it, that's the trouble. He was dressed rough, in jeans and a bomber-jacket, not the way he used to dress at the office. But I'm pretty sure. I almost stopped the car, then I realised it might be dangerous. Coming back, I drove quite slowly, but there wasn't any sign of him then. I rang Mr Hastings. He told me to sleep on it, unless I was absolutely positive. But I couldn't get it out of my mind. I felt I had to let you know.'

Gently fiddled with the pipe. 'You haven't been that way since?'

'No – I mean ... If he recognised me ...'

8

'So it was just that single sighting. As you were driving by in your car.'

'Yes, I suppose so. But why would I think it was him, if it wasn't?'

'At the moment, Thorpe is on everyone's mind.'

'But not just then – not on mine.'

Gently sighed to himself again. In the past fortnight there had been numerous alleged sightings of the missing accountant, mostly in the city, where he had probably gone to earth, but others from as far afield as Birmingham. The case had made headlines. His picture had been published, been issued to every police station in the land. And Shinglebourne was surely one of the least likely of places where he might have tucked himself away . . .

'Miss Ford?'

'Yes – I'm still here.'

'I have to thank you for reporting this matter. But what I would ask you to do now is to pass it on to the local police, who will take whatever steps are necessary. Would you be kind enough to do that?'

'Yes, but I thought, since you were in charge . . .'

'Thank you for calling, Miss Ford.'

'Yes, but I thought . . .'

Gently hung up. He rang the bell for Dutt. 'Did you hear all that?'

'Yes, sir. And a right old tale I thought it was.'

'Still, give Shinglebourne a ring.'

'Right you are sir, just to be safe. Perhaps chummie knew Shinglebourne when he was a nipper and never thought we'd dream of looking for him there.'

Well – it was possible. Gently refilled his pipe and applied himself again to the report on his desk.


But he read and countersigned it mechanically, frowning as he dropped it in his out-tray. For some days now he had been trying to put the Hastings case behind him. It was cut and dried. No questions remained about the culprit and his probable motive; they needed only to lay their hands on him to wrap it up. And yet . . . He shook his head, got up and went to stare out of the window, at the cranes, at the traffic below, at the slowly turning sign in the courtyard.

It had begun with a ring from Tanner, the Chelsea Detective Chief Inspector.

'Sir, we've got a stiff here in a flat in Putney, which we think should have your attention.'

'A stiff?'

'Seems she's the wife of a business tycoon in Fulham. He reported her missing yesterday. They've got a villa near the Windmill on Wimbledon Common.'

'So what was she doing in Putney?'

'Visiting her toy-boy it looks like, sir.'

'And what does he say?'

'Doesn't say nothing, sir. As far as we can tell he's done a flit.'

'I'll be right along.'

With Dutt driving, they had wended their way there from the Yard, to a pleasant basement flat in a block that, at the rear, overlooked the Thames. An ambulance was backed in on the paved parking from which steps descended to a sheltered area adorned with plants in tubs, and through the open door they could see flashes of light as the camera crew went about their business.

Tanner met them at the door. 'One for the Sunday papers, sir.'

'Has the victim's identity been confirmed?'

'Yes, sir. We fetched her old man here. But he was pretty sick, as you can imagine, so I had him driven back to his office.'

'Exactly who is he?'

'Name of Hastings, sir. He owns a big advertising firm in Fulham. And the geezer who owns this flat works for him. He's an accountant, name of Thorpe.'

'And he was her lover?'

'That's how it looks, sir. We've asked around and she's

10

often been seen visiting the flat. She's younger than her old man and I dare say she found him a bit dull.'

'Did he know about it?'

'I hardly liked to ask him. But we can talk to him at the office.'

'What brought you here looking for her?'

Tanner shook his head. 'It was Thorpe we came here looking for, sir. We got a call to say he hadn't turned up for work and that someone had cleaned out the office safe. Then we got here and found what we found, and remembered that the lady had been reported missing. Hastings last saw her at lunch-time yesterday, but when he got home later she wasn't there. He rang her brother at Chelsea and some people they knew, and then he got worried and rang us.'

'Have we an ETD?'

'A rough one, sir. Between two and five the doc says.'

'Between two and five . . .'

Tanner nodded eagerly. 'And that puts the toy-boy right on the spot. His boss asked him to work late on a costing job, which was coming in that afternoon, so he gave him time off to make up for it. He was out of the office from two-ish till five.'

'So . . . he rang the lady?'

'That's my guess. And she came here hotfoot from Wimbledon. What happened after that we don't know, but it finished up with her lying strangled on the bed.'

On the bed. Yvonne Hastings. With her eyes still staring terror. A slim woman, perhaps five foot four, with delicate features and dark shoulder-length hair. Dressed in an expensive two-piece and a frilled blouse. With unmistakable bruising on her throat. No apparent struggle or interference. And her handbag lying by her side.

'You've checked the bag?'

'She hadn't been robbed, sir. No need, when chummie had the keys to the safe.'

'Anything suggestive discovered in the flat?'

11

'Just some letters from his relatives. His mother lives in Reading and he's got a married sister in Sevenoaks. I've been on the phone to the locals and they're going to ring back when they've done a check. Oh . . . and there's this.'

He produced a photograph. It showed a couple with their arms about each other's waists. The woman was clearly Yvonne Hastings. Her companion, a good-looking young man with his hair worn in a style.

'Thorpe?'

'Jason Thorpe, sir. I showed the photograph to her old man and that was when he nearly threw up. Like you can see, it was taken here in the flat, using a camera with delayed exposure. We've got some other good snaps of him if we need to issue a picture.'

He produced them also. No question, Jason Thorpe was an attractive fellow. In his early thirties, square, well-balanced features, amused hazel eyes, the styled hair golden-brown. The picture of a killer . . .? Who could tell? First, one needed to know the degree of provocation.

'What do you reckon, sir?'

Gently shook his head. They would perhaps never know what had triggered that violence. Meanwhile, the photographers had finished their job and the ambulance men were standing by with a stretcher. Elsewhere other members of Tanner's team were proceeding with the examination of the flat. A desirable flat with its view of the river . . . why hadn't Thorpe dumped the body in the Thames?

'Let's talk to Hastings.'

The offices, off Fulham Broadway, would only have been a twenty-minute walk from the flat; extensive premises with ultra-modern furnishings and a neon sign over the entrance. They were shown through to a large office luxuriously carpeted and equipped. There sat, or rather huddled, a smartly suited man, at a period mahogany desk, near his elbow an empty glass and, sitting beside him, a solemn-faced blonde. The latter rose as though to leave them, but the man signalled her back to her seat.

'Mr Oswald Hastings?'

He merely nodded.

'Chief Superintendent Gently. Chief Inspector Tanner you have already met.'

Another nod.

'First, let me express our sympathy for the tragic occurrence that brings us here. If it were possible we would be only too happy to postpone this interview till a later occasion, but unfortunately it is necessary for us to obtain information at the earliest opportunity.'

'I understand.'

A growling voice. A tall, well-built man of around fifty. Thinning grey hair, a bald spot, full features, bold brown eyes. He stared wretchedly at Gently, then glanced towards the empty glass. 'So what is it you want to know?'

'Whatever you can tell us about yesterday.'

'Yesterday . . .'

'I understand you last saw your wife at lunch-time.'

'At . . . lunch-time.' He scowled at the desk. 'Christine, pour me another one.'

The blonde, presumably his secretary, hastened to take the glass and to refill it from a decanter at a miniature bar.

He received it ungraciously, coughed and drank, then stared back at Gently. 'You were saying?'

'You had your lunch at home?'

'Yes. I usually have my lunch at home.'

'And everything appeared normal?'

'Yes. Normal. Just lunch like any other day.'

'Did your wife mention any plan she had for the afternoon?'

'Yvonne rarely bothered to tell me her plans.'

'You were not in her confidence?'

'If you want to put it that way. I should think it's pretty obvious now.'

Gently paused. 'I'm sorry to have to ask you this, but had you no suspicion of your wife's infidelity?'

'I – perhaps.' He took another drink. 'Yes,' he said. 'Yes. Just lately. We . . . we were never that close. I was perhaps a fool ever to have married her. My first wife left me for another man and I married Yvonne on the rebound. Five years ago. It started off all right, but then it seemed to drift a little. It may be I was too old for her – that's what her brother thought. But we still got along all right until, well, I suppose the last few weeks.' He drank. 'She wanted her own room, said that my snoring kept her awake. I let her have her way, but I began to wonder, was half thinking of having an eye kept on her.'

'But you didn't do that?'

He shook his head.

'And you didn't suspect who the man might be?'

His head shook again. 'Thorpe I thought I could trust. He's been with us four years and has always given good service.'

'How would she have met him?'

'Here, in the office. She would bring in some bill she wanted me to pay and I would send her to him to take care of it. Christine can tell you.'

The blonde secretary blushed and gave a nervous nod.

'Right,' Gently said. 'So we'll get back to yesterday. At what time did you leave home again for the office?'

'At around one thirty.'

'And Thorpe was here when you arrived?'

'Thorpe was here.'

'But then you released him for the afternoon, because you required him to work later that day/evening?'

'It sometimes happens. One of our clients is Windows, the computer firm, and they were planning their campaign for next year. They wanted a costing at the earliest and promised to deliver a rough before closing. As a matter of fact' – he scowled at the glass – 'the details were here soon after Thorpe left, but it was too late then, so we let it stand as arranged.'

'And he left – when?'

'Around two.'

'And returned?'

Hastings glanced at the blonde.

14

'It was just before closing, sir!' she faltered. 'It would have been half past five.'

Gently said: 'You spoke to him?'

'Yes. He came to me for the documents.'

'He seemed quite normal?'

'Yes, I think so.'

'I spoke to him too,' Hastings growled. 'Looked in at his office as we were packing up ... my God, if I'd known what I know now.'

'But nothing struck you then?'

He shook his head and tossed back the last of his drink.

'So,' Gently said. 'Thorpe arrived at the office and apparently made a start on the task he'd been given. Would he have continued with it?'

Hastings stared. 'Yes. I found it on my desk this morning.'

'He was still trying to act normally, you'd say?'

'I suppose so. Oh lord, I shall never understand it.'

'As though, at that time, he might still have had other plans.'

'Other plans . . .?'

'Forgive me. But his flat is very close to the river.'

'The river . . .' Hastings kept staring, then he jerked his face away. 'Please. Please! I don't think I can take this. Not on top of all the rest.'

'I'm sorry,' Gently said. 'But we have to understand his actions. If he had such a plan, he clearly abandoned it. And it wouldn't have worked. There was too much against him. He decided that flight was his best option.'

'So for heaven's sake – !'

'How long would it have taken him to complete his task?'

'Three hours. Four. I don't know. He could have been here till midnight.'

'And the keys of the safe – he would have those?'

'I don't give a rap about the rotten money.'

'But you would know apporoximately how much was in there?'

15

'No, it wasn't my pigeon. Ask Christine.'

The blonde had been snivelling; she dabbed her eyes with a tissue.

'Well?' Gently said.

'Three or four thousand . . . the clerk, Mr Cohen, worked it out.'

'In small notes?'

'Yes, I think. They were all we had any use for.'

Gently nodded. Thorpe was well-equipped, had the means to tuck himself away out of sight. But where to begin looking was the next question, to what haven might the fugitive have directed his flight . . .?

Gently addressed the blonde. 'You will have Thorpe's details?'

'Yes, of course.'

She fetched the sheet from a filing cabinet. Apart from the mother at her address in Reading it recorded no other relative. His references mentioned an accountant in Roe-hampton with whom, presumably, he had served his apprenticeship. Friends? The blonde was uncertain. Leisure occupations? She shook her head. Had he mentioned holidays? Once, she remembered, he had talked of a climbing holiday in Scotland. It didn't sound hopeful and, while they were discussing it, Hastings poured himself another drink from the decanter . . .

So, they were duly thanked for their co-operation and advised that statements would be required; appropriate orders were issued and a break declared for lunch.

A sad business. And the weather was matching it, with last night's rain beginning again – rain that must have accompanied the missing accountant as he fled with his well-lined pockets. He had no car. Had he taken the Tube? Prudence would warn him not to call a taxi and the Tube could land him at a main-line station with access to any point in the compass – or, it might be, a suburban stop and some obscure hotel or boarding-house . . .

'Shouldn't take us long, sir – chummie isn't a pro.'

In the afternoon calls began to come in. The mother had

seen nothing of Thorpe in Reading, nor the married sister in Sevenoaks, though the latter was able to provide the information that he occasionally spent weekends with a friend in Eastbourne. His picture and description were circulated, and a press conference was called at the Yard. And an item of information arrived from Forensic that might, or might not, have a bearing on the tragedy. For two months, perhaps three, Yvonne Hastings had been pregnant . . .

'That's it, sir.'

Well . . . it was credible.

'She was aiming to cut loose and go and live with Thorpe. But he wouldn't wear it. And maybe she threatened him, said she'd tell Hastings and get him sacked.'

'The child could have been Hastings's.'

'It isn't likely, sir. They had been married for five years. And remember how he told us she had stopped sleeping with him – it would have been about when she discovered she was pregnant.'

Yes. It fitted. She was pregnant by her lover, had perhaps broken it to him at that fatal meeting, had sworn she couldn't go back to her husband, had pleaded to be allowed to stay with him.

And Thorpe . . .

'Get Hastings on the phone.'

A shocked silence was Hastings's first reaction.

'You knew nothing of it?'

'Oh lord – no! And to think she never told me . . .'

So that was that: when it came to court, motive to add to opportunity. All that remained was to feel his shoulder and that, surely, could not be long delayed.

'Check whether he had been issued with a passport.'

No such document had been found at the flat. There, the signs were of a hasty departure: drawers left open, clothes tossed aside. A bank statement revealed a well-furnished account, but for the moment he would have no need to draw on that . . .

'Yes, sir, they say he did have one.'

'Take the usual action.'

'Right, sir.'

Ports, airports, the Tunnel. But intuition was against it. Always, town seemed the likeliest area of search, the place where, they had learned, he had been born and brought up, and where, since, he had lived and worked. He knew London. In the rain of the night, familiar places would have been his goal; a refuge more distant might come later. For the moment, their search was best directed in town.

Next day the papers and the phone calls.

'They are holding this fellow in Dover, sir . . .'

Then it was Lewes and Tunbridge Wells, and a likely prospect in Eastbourne.

'Have you seen the *Sun*, sir?'

On the front page was a picture of a young man who wasn't Thorpe, but the victim's brother, one Christopher Norton, an estate agent domiciled in Chelsea. An angry young man. LET ME GET MY HANDS ON HIM! was the caption that went with the picture and in the interview that accompanied it appeared other vengeful intimations.

'Tell someone to have a word with him.'

All day the phone calls poured in. And the next day. And the next. But then they grew fewer, while the story had drifted from the front page.

A phone call from Chiswick might have reinstated it: 'Sir, we've pulled this body out of the river.'

A credible body, answering the description, and one that sent Tanner haring out to Chiswick. But alack and alas, he arrived there to find a sobbing young woman in the police-station reception. The body was her husband's, no possible doubt, she could describe an operation scar on its stomach . . .

'I don't know, sir. The way it's going, he might well be dead. It's a week, now, and not a smell of him. You would think we were looking for a ghost.'

A week and rapidly becoming a fortnight – it shaped like a case that was heading for the files. Other scraps of information were rounded up, but nothing that gave them a lead to the fugitive. Testimony from the doctor who had confirmed the pregnancy, a broken appointment with a hairdresser on the vital afternoon, sightings of the victim in the company of Thorpe, though none at a time that would have been useful. Meanwhile other business, other crimes . . . until . . . and unless?

'Shinglebourne for you, sir.'

Gently turned from the window to pick up the phone. 'Gently here.'

'Beamish, sir. I thought I'd better give you a ring . . .'

DI Beamish, the chubby-faced Shinglebourne I/c, whom Gently had done business with before.

'The lady reported to you?'

'Oh yes, sir. But she didn't seem any too sure of her facts. And the truth is there's a layabout called Dyball who's been dossing out there, in the old coach.'

'Who answers the description?'

'Could do, sir, though he's older than the bloke you're looking for. I've sent a patrol out there, but I thought I'd let you know the odds.'

Gently pulled a face. 'Thanks, Beamish.'

'I'll ring you back if there's anything to report, sir.'

Another bum steer . . .

He selected a fresh pipe and got back to the documents in his in-tray. One case among many – get it out of his mind. Crimes didn't dry up because of one missing client. He worked steadily through the rest of the morning, with only occasional interruptions, and it wasn't until he was leaving for lunch that the phone rang again.

'Shinglebourne, sir.'

'Beamish?'

'Sir, I don't know quite how to tell you this.'

Beamish sounded on edge; in the background was what sounded like hysterical sobbing.

'You found a man at the coach?'

'Yes – we did.'

'And it wasn't Thorpe?'

'That's just the point, sir. We think it is, but the lady here still can't swear it's him . . .'

'Let me speak to her.'

'Don't think you can, sir. She's in a state.'

'But she must be able to identify him.'

'Sir, that's the trouble . . . he's been bashed about.'

'You mean?'

'Dead, sir. That's how we found him. Lying on an old bedstead with his head battered in. Cold and stiff. According to Dr Capel he'd been dead for at least six hours.'

'Battered to death.'

'We've got the weapon, a rusty poker . . .'

'And no identification?'

'None we've found, sir. That's why we took the lady along.'

'A wallet – a passport?'

'Nothing, sir. Just a suitcase with some clothes – underwear, a smart two-piece, and a toilet bag and gear.'

Gently stared hard at the cranes. 'If it's Thorpe, he would have had money in his possession. Three thousand pounds or more. Have you conducted a search of the coach?'

'Not yet, sir. But we're on it now. Do you reckon the odds are it's him?'

Yes. The odds were very strong.

'Send his prints in straight away. We can match them with those found in his flat.'

'Shall we be seeing you, sir?'

'If the prints match you'll be seeing me later today.'

He hung up. Shinglebourne . . . Was there any way of tying Thorpe to it? He pulled out the case file and found the number of the sister in Sevenoaks.

'Mrs Fowler? Chief Superintendent Gently. I'm wondering if you can provide me with some information . . .'

She could. When she and her brother were children, they had twice been on holiday with their parents at Shinglebourne, at the time of the Festival – her father had been an opera buff. She would know the town well? Oh yes. The

20

old railway coach? They used to play round it. Had they . . . news of her brother there, then? Perhaps later. He hung up.

After that, the matching of the prints seemed almost superfluous.

'Fetch me my overnight bag, Dutt.'

'So we're off to the seaside, sir!'

Gabrielle he didn't need to ring: his wife was away at her business in distant Rouen.

# 2

Shinglebourne, when he arrived there in the late afternoon, seemed the least likely of settings for a gory murder. Banners decked the main street, the shops were lavish with special displays, promenade and pavements were crowded with Festival-goers and there was scarcely a vacant parking space in the town. The Festival was a famous occasion. Enthusiasts gathered there from the Continent and further afield. Everywhere one saw cars with foreign plates and in restaurants heard the babble of foreign tongues . . .

At the police station he was obliged to double-park. Beamish and his sergeant, Bidwell, were waiting for him and ushered him through to the former's office, where, laid out on a table, were a suitcase and its contents – a business suit, shirts, underwear and the basic articles of toilet. Also . . . a passport in the name of Jason Reginald Thorpe.

'Where did you find this?'

Beamish looked guilty. 'It's just come to light, sir. He'd stuffed it away behind the lining in his suitcase and we only found it a minute ago.'

'And the money?'

Beamish shook his head. 'Some loose change in the pocket of the jeans he was wearing. We turned that old coach inside out, but there was no trace of anything else.'

'No sign of his wallet?'

'No, sir. And if he had a watch that was gone too.'

'Any unidentified prints?'

'A few of them, sir. And a bit of a smudge on the poker. But it was an old, rusty job and we've sent it off to Forensic, along with the clothes he had on. He was living rough and sleeping under sacks on an old iron bedstead that lies there. That's where we found him. He never had a chance, chummie must have struck him before he could move.'

'Have you the photographs?'

'Just come in, sir.'

The prints were still reeking of printing fluid. From what they showed it was not surprising that the secretary couldn't swear to an identity. The bloody face had been almost pulped, with the sodden hair glued to the sacking below it. Other pictures showed the sacks turned back and the body clad in jeans and a vest. Almost certainly Thorpe would have been asleep when the vicious attack had been made . . .

Beamish was studying the prints alongside Gently. 'Chummie wasn't taking any chances, sir. I reckon one of those whacks would have laid the bloke out, there was no need to carry on like that. Do you think we're dealing with a psycho?'

'It's possible.'

'It's like he couldn't stop himself, once he'd begun. Just had to keep bashing him. Though it didn't stop him from running off with the poor sod's wallet. He really had a ball.'

Gently shrugged.

'Could have been he knew about the dough,' Beamish said. 'He may have been keeping an eye on the bloke, perhaps saw him with his wallet out down at the shops.'

'Any prospects on the books?'

'A few wild ones, sir. There's drugs around here like everywhere else.'

'One in particular?'

Beamish thought, but shook his head. 'Not one I'd think capable of a job like that. More like, it would be some bastard passing through, perhaps up here to see if there were pickings at the Festival. We get some of those.'

'And?'

'Just a dip, whom Bidwell picked up two days ago.'

Gently laid the prints aside. 'So now we'll take a look at the scene of the crime. My information is that Thorpe was familiar with it, may have headed there directly when he fled from town. Have any other sightings of him come to light yet?'

'Not yet, sir. But we'll keep trying.'

'Most especially we'd like to know if he's been seen in the company of any other person.'

Beamish nodded. And led the way to the cars.


Tapes stretched along the verge before the ancient coach, that relic of a line now only a memory, and a uniformed man stood guarding it from a collection of bystanders in the road.

A camera fizzed as Gently climbed from the car and a reporter thrust a microphone towards him. 'Chief Superintendent Gently, sir?'

'Later, boys.'

'But could you just tell us – was it the man you were looking for?'

'We believe the victim to be Jason Thorpe.'

'And you think – ?'

'There'll be a statement later.'

He pushed the reporter aside and followed Beamish through the tapes. The coach was sited some fifty yards from the road, on rough land devoted to scrub and brambles. Back down the road the town ended at the old Moot Hall and the White Hart Hotel, and in the other direction, two miles off, appeared the cluster of houses that was Holmeness. Then, across the road, the beach and the sea, the latter pale and sparkling in the afternoon sun, and to the rear the flat plain of salt marsh, stretching to distant trees and higher ground.

'Not a bad spot for a hide-out, sir.'

No. It was merest chance that had run Thorpe to earth. Had there been no Festival to attract the secretary, he might well have remained safe till the first phase of the hunt was over. And then . . . with Harwich just down the road, and the passport they'd found tucked away in his suitcase?

The coach was one of the pre-war Third Class type that one entered only by doors at either end, and which, a long time since, had been adapted as some sort of dwelling. The compartments had been removed, most windows blanked with plywood and a stove with a chimney fitted. Then there was a crude sink, beside which was a pump, the rusting bedstead and little else. On the latter were sacks stuffed with bracken: the one at the head end bearing stains. Lighting? Tossed aside, an old oil-lamp. Toilet? An Elsan, standing proud in a corner.

'I reckon the winter would have winkled him out, sir.'

Shelterless, the coach stood to the sea: to the east wind and the winter storms, of which its weathered timber bore ample evidence. It was probably its exposed situation that had led to its abandonment in the first place.

'And your search was thorough?'

'Every last nook, sir. I even had a bloke scramble round underneath. And those brambles outside, we poked through them. If the cash had been there we must have found it.'

'You mentioned a layabout who used to sleep here.'

'Dyball, sir. A fellow in his fifties. He comes this way every summer and lives off begging. We've had to talk to him.'

'He lives rough?'

'I'll say! He comes out from Eastwich, whom I've had a word with. Seems his marriage broke up a few years back and he's been on the streets ever since.'

'Any record?'

Beamish shook his head.

'And he's around now?'

'Oh yes, he's around.'

'Only . . . not sleeping here?'

Beamish thought about it, but then shook his head again. 'I know he does use this place, sir, but I can't swear he's been here lately. He might well have been dossing in town, with the sort of weather we've had lately.'

'He could have information.'

26

'We'll talk to him, sir. But anything else, I don't think it's on. Dyball isn't the type. He's a quiet sort of bloke, who wouldn't cut up rough with anybody.'

Gently shrugged, filled a pipe and stared at the stains on the sacking. He was feeling puzzled, still, by the viciousness, the violence of that killing. A psychopathic robber? It was not impossible, the two characters might sometimes mix. But failing that? Or a revengeful beggar, who had been slung out of his adopted abode? He lit his pipe. 'We'll have to step up the questioning. Anyone who saw Thorpe, who may have spoken to him, especially in the last few days, or who was anywhere near here this morning. We'll issue an appeal in the press and on local radio.'

'I was going to suggest it, sir.'

'Apart from that – '

They were interrupted by the arrival of one of Beamish's men, towing behind him another man, dressed in the slop and cap of a fisherman.

'Sir, there's someone here who might have seen something – he's often at the net store just across the road.'

His name was Bircham, a long-shoreman of sturdy build and weathered features. On one occasion ten days earlier he had been repairing a net at the hut on the beach – he pointed it out, a small timber building, perhaps a hundred and fifty yards distant from the coach.

'You saw the man who was living here?'

'Reckon I did. A young feller in jeans and one of those jackets. I've seen him about here since, but that's the only time he had someone with him.'

'Someone – you can identify?'

'Blast, yes. I've seen *him* around here enough. An old bloke who lives rough and who's always touching you for a pint. I dare say you'll know who I mean.'

'You saw him in company with the other man?'

'Ah. I saw them come out of here together. Stood nattering for a bit, they did, but too far off for me to hear what they said. Then this young feller feels in his pocket – I could guess what was going on then. I nearly hollered to him not to be a fool, but there you are. There's one born every minute.'

'He gave him money?'

'He bloody did. And it wasn't just the price of a pint. It was his wallet he pulled out and I saw a couple of notes change hands.'

'A couple of notes . . .'

'Ah. Twenty quid he gave that bloke. Then he waves him away and comes back in here, and the old boy makes off for the nearest pub.'

'And that was the only time you have seen them together?'

'Yes, that one time.'

'And you've seen no one else with the younger man?'

'No.' Bircham paused. 'You don't reckon . . .?'

'Thank you, Mr Bircham,' Gently said. 'We shall require your written statement, so I must ask you to accompany this officer to the police station.'

Bircham shook his head. 'I can't believe that,' he said. 'No, I can't believe it . . .'

He was ushered out. Beamish stared at Gently. 'Not sure I can believe it either, sir,' he said. 'But if Thorpe was flashing his dough like that it might have started giving Dyball ideas. What do you say?'

Gently shrugged. 'Perhaps we will know more when we've talked to Dyball. Will you round him up?'

'You bet. His feet aren't going to touch, sir.'

The scene had little more to offer and shortly they returned to the car, fending off a fresh attempt by the reporter, who had been excited by the departure of the fisherman apparently under guard . . .


'Name?'

'Samuel Dyball.'

'Address?'

'You can put what you like.'

'Occupation?'

28

'Just call me retired.'

'Age?'

'Your guess is as good as mine.'

They had only to wait at the office for half an hour before the down-and-out was marched in, a figure in a soiled coat, ragged trousers and scuffed, down-at-heel shoes. His greying hair was long and tangled, and his face half hidden in a bush of beard. He was certainly nervous. He stood before them uneasily, his grey eyes squinting from one to the other.

'Turn out your pockets, Dyball.'

'Well, if you say so.'

Out came a medley of rubbish, but which included with it a pack of cigarettes, a handful of change and a five-pound note.

Beamish pointed to the last. 'Where did this come from?'

'A bloke give it to me, didn't he?'

'He gave you a fiver?'

'Yes, one of them foreigners. I dare say he didn't know much about our money.'

'You're sure that's who gave it to you?'

'Course I am.'

Beamish stared at him, then shook his head. 'Sit down, Dyball.'

A chair was placed for him before the desk and Dyball sat. A man probably around fifty but, from his occupation, looking ten years older. A strong frame under the shapeless coat. Roughened, but useful-looking hands. A man who could probably take care of himself if the occasion should call for it.

'Now,' Beamish said. 'Now, Dyball. You'll know what happened up at the old coach last night. The old coach where you've been dossing. So where were you last night, Dyball?'

'Me? I wasn't nowhere near – '

'So where were you?'

'Me – ?'

'You, Dyball.'

29

'I tell you!' There was fear in his eyes. 'I was down here in the town – in that shelter on the front.'

'Which shelter?'

'That one near the lifeboat. Ask anyone. That's where I've been sleeping.'

'And you can prove that's where you were?'

'Yes – I don't know. You ask them.'

Beamish dealt him a hard stare. 'Now you listen to me, Dyball. You've been dossing in that coach every time you've come this way. You were there a fortnight ago. But then this smart young fellow turns up. And he doesn't want to share with someone like you, so you get slung out of your coach. A young man, Dyball, with his pocket full of notes. Notes that vanished some time last night.'

'But it wasn't me. I never knew – '

'You are going to tell me you didn't know he was loaded?'

'No. How could I?'

'There's one easy way.'

'No, I thought – '

Beamish shook his head.

'I tell you.' Now the fear was too apparent. He was hot and sweating behind the beard, eyes wide, hands working.

'We have a witness, Dyball.'

'No!'

'Someone who saw you and the young man together.'

'They couldn't – '

'Someone who knows you. Whom you've touched for a pint before now.'

'No. No!' He dragged his gaze from Beamish, stared down at his tormented hands. 'All right, he did give me a tip to clear out – there's nothing wrong with that, is there? Told me he'd come up for the Festival and couldn't find a room anywhere in town.'

'He told you that?'

'It's true!'

'And then he pulls out his fat wallet?'

'He give me a tenner – '

30

'Oh dear,' Beamish said.

'All right then – it was a couple.'

'A couple,' Beamish said. 'From that very fat wallet. Which somehow he managed to keep invisible.'

'But I didn't know – !'

'Listen,' Beamish said. 'Your little eyes would have seen that wallet. It was stuffed. It had to be. The young man had three thousand nicker along with him. And this morning what do we find? We find that young man lying dead on the bed. No wallet. No bundles of cash. Just the loose change he had in his pocket. And who was it knew he had the dough? If you try to tell me different I'll spit.'

'But it wasn't – it wasn't me!'

'Dyball, you knew about that money.'

'I know, but I didn't – I wasn't – '

Beamish turned his eyes to the ceiling.

After a pause, Gently said: 'You knew the young man had money, there can be no doubt about that. And yet, he seemed content to be living rough in a derelict coach outside the town. Wouldn't that have struck you as a little odd?'

'He told me why he was doing that.'

Gently nodded. 'For the first week, perhaps, but afterwards wouldn't you have thought it strange? By the weekend there could have been rooms available, but he seemed to have made no effort to book one.'

'Well, I don't know. These youngsters . . .'

'I think it may have occurred to you,' Gently said. 'A young man with a load of money, preferring to live obscurely out there. A subject for conversation perhaps. When you were spending his money at the bar.'

'No – I never mentioned it.'

'He warned you not to?'

'Well – '

'Did he?'

Dyball writhed in the chair. 'So if he did, what was the harm in that?'

'He offered you more money to keep a still tongue?'

31

Dyball said nothing.

'A tenner now and then?'

'Oh . . . bugger it!' Dyball stared defiantly. 'When you're in my shoes, you can't turn up a deal like that. Nor I never knew what he'd been up to. It didn't have to be you lot who was on his tail.'

'To you, he was just a source of income.'

'Put it like that if you want to.'

'And you never spoke about him to a soul.'

'Why would I be mug enough to do that?'

Gently nodded. 'One other thing. Did you ever see him in the company of other people?'

Dyball thought about it. 'Just shopping, like. When he come into town to buy some grub.'

'But he spoke to nobody in particular?'

'Not that I ever saw. For the most part he stuck around the coach, or maybe he'd take a stroll up the beach.'

'But always alone?'

'Like I say.' Dyball frowned. 'He never did strike me as a wrong'un,' he said. 'Just a nice young bloke, kind of well-to-do. Who was it after him? Was it his wife?'

'Thank you, Dyball,' Gently said. He glanced at Beamish, who merely shrugged. 'That will be all for the present, except that we shall require your written statement and a set of your fingerprints.'

'My prints? But – bloody hell!'

'Just routine,' Gently said.

'But you can't really think – !'

'This officer will attend to you.'


Bidwell shepherded Dyball out and they could hear his complaining voice in the office next door. Gently lit his pipe.

Beamish went for a moment to stare at the window. Then he returned to the desk. 'So what are we going to make of that, sir?'

Gently puffed a few times. 'I think we shall need to look further than Dyball,' he said.

'I don't know, sir.' Beamish felt for a fag. 'He was almost shopping himself just now. By his account, it was only him who had dealings with Thorpe and knew about the cash. To the best of my knowledge he's never been violent, but you have to admit the temptation was there, sir. And the way it was done, that wasn't professional. More like a rush of blood in some amateur.'

'Yes . . . the way it was done.'

'An amateur job. The sort you would have to expect from him. And he's got no alibi. He may have slept in the shelter, but the job wasn't done till daybreak this morning. He could have slunk up there first thing and done it, and nobody any the wiser.'

Gently puffed. 'And the money?'

'Oh, he'd have found some cache for that, sir. He'd know better than to carry it on him and he's familiar with all the odd places round here.' Beamish paused. 'So what do you reckon, sir?'

Gently shook his head. 'Just that we'd better put Dyball on hold. He didn't have to kill Thorpe, he was on Thorpe's payroll and Thorpe couldn't afford not to come across. And of this Dyball seems to have been well aware. He could have stuck out for any pay-off he fancied.'

'But not the whole shute, sir!'

'Even that. Just remember what it was that Thorpe was running away from.'

Beamish puffed frowningly. 'So – no action with Dyball, sir?'

'I think not for the moment. Until we've made the usual round of enquiries. And unless, by an outside chance, a print of his matches the one on the poker.'

'I still can't help fancying him, sir.'

Gently shrugged and struck his pipe a fresh light.

There was no match. The prints taken from Dyball fitted those found everywhere in the coach, but that on the poker

33

was too smudged to allow a certain comparison to be made. Regretfully, Beamish returned Dyball's possessions and permitted the down-and-out to depart – with a suitable warning. And, on second thoughts, with one of his DCs on Dyball's tail.

'The dough, sir – he won't stray far from that.'

Then followed an encounter with the press, with lively questions and suppositions to be dealt with and suppressed . . .

'The old fellow who was here, sir – was he able to assist you?'

'No comment.'

'The fisherman . . .?'

'Ditto.'

'The lady who was here – can we have her address?'

'Her business had no direct connection with the crime.'

Finally they were dismissed to their cars and mobile phones, when, other than an occasional report being filed, the proceedings lapsed into a hiatus.

'Time for a meal.'

They left Bidwell in the office and Gently steered Beamish towards the White Hart. As usual at the time of the Festival the hotel was packed with customers and they were fortunate to arrive in the restaurant just as a table was being vacated. They ordered pints and took their seats. Outside, strollers still occupied the promenade, many proceeding towards the coast road, where, a short distance further on . . .

'Look, sir. Over there!'

Gently glanced in the direction indicated. Seated at a table across the room was the blonde secretary, Christine Ford. She was in the company of another woman who was addressing her in earnest conversation, but apparently with little result. Christine Ford sat silent and wretched. Then her eye caught Gently's. She started and looked away.

'You'll have met her back in town, sir?'

Gently nodded.

'Still looks knocked up,' Beamish said. 'I thought we'd

have to call a stretcher for her, the way she was carrying on.' He paused, frowning. 'No connection was there, sir – I mean her and the bloke back there?'

'None that we know of.'

'Well, the way she behaved! It wasn't a pretty sight, I can tell you. But it could have been her husband or boy-friend lying there, the amount of fuss she was making.'

'Thorpe was the lover of the woman found dead in his flat.'

'Yes, sir. But there could have been an earlier connection.'

'If so, then it's all one now.'

'I suppose so, sir.'

Beamish sighed and took a pull at his glass.

But they hadn't quite finished with Christine Ford. At the coffee stage she rose and came over to their table.

'If I may . . .'

'Please sit, Miss Ford.'

'It's just that I – '

'Do take a seat.'

Nervously, she sat and tried to compose herself. Tears streaked her make-up. Across at the other table her friend was keenly watching the encounter.

At last Miss Ford's flickering blue eyes found Gently's. 'I feel so responsible,' she said. 'If only I hadn't waited, but had told you yesterday, this terrible thing wouldn't have happened. But I couldn't convince myself it was Jason I'd seen in such an unlikely place.' Her mouth twisted. 'I suppose . . .?'

Slowly Gently nodded. 'I'm afraid there can be no doubt, Miss Ford.'

'Oh, it's dreadful!' She hung her head. 'I asked Madge – that's my friend – what I should do and even rang my boss. If only I hadn't been such a fool! They both thought it improbable I would have seen him here, though, in my heart of hearts . . .'

'You knew him very well, Miss Ford?'

She gestured with her head.

'Had you any suspicion of the affair he was engaged in?'

35

'Please, don't ask me.'

'But . . .?'

'Oh, I may have had an idea. But nothing I could put my finger on. Just the way she used to hang around his office.'

'Nothing you felt you should mention to Mr Hastings?'

'Oh lord, no! I wouldn't have dared to. Anyway, he had his own ideas about that, though I don't know if he knew who the fellow was – otherwise, Jason would have been sacked.' She whimpered. 'And now . . .'

'You mustn't blame yourself, Miss Ford.'

'But perhaps both times . . . if I'd spoken up . . .'

'It was unfortunate. But you're not to blame.'

She snatched a tissue from her sleeve and dabbed away tears. 'But . . . who could have done such a thing?' she snivelled. 'It was terrible! Jason may have asked for trouble, but he didn't deserve anything like this. Do you know who did it?'

'We are taking every step.'

'A man like that . . . he could do it again.'

'Rest assured, Miss Ford, we'll leave no stone unturned. And now my advice to you is that you have an early night.'

'You too? That's what Madge says. But how I'm ever going to sleep again . . .'

Unsteadily, she rose and left them, to seek the consolation of her concerned-looking friend; and together they departed up the hotel stairs to where, presumably, they had quarters.

Beamish lit a thoughtful fag. 'See what I mean about her, sir?' he said. 'She's taking it a bit too hard. I still fancy she had an eye for that bloke.'

Gently shrugged. 'I suppose it's possible.'

There was a gleam in Beamish's eye. 'And she's quite a tidy looker. If it wasn't for her at home, I wouldn't mind having a secretary like that.'

## 3

Other than Dyball, who could have been aware of that
dangerous sum in the stranger's possession?

'It keeps adding up, sir.'

But Gently shook his head – what need had the down-
and-out to commit such a deed? He had Thorpe weighed
up. To preserve his obscurity the young man was always
ready to dip into the stuffed wallet ... already it was at
Dyball's command; there could be no reason for a step so
drastic.

'He may have let something slip to a third party.'

'It's possible, sir. But I can't think he would. Dyball's a
loner. And it was against his interest to shoot his mouth off
about Thorpe.'

'His being in funds may have aroused curiosity. His
applications to Thorpe could have been observed.'

'If you say so, sir.'

'We should perhaps be watching out for a likely client
who seems to be suddenly well-heeled.'

Beamish looked doubtful. 'I'll put it about, sir. But off-
hand there's no one who comes to mind. We've got our
quota, like everyone else, but I can't think of one for a job
like this. If it were a mugging, now. Or a dip.'

Yes; the ferocity remained a problem. If there had been
no complication of theft ... But even the victim's wrist-
watch had vanished.

'Maybe we'll hear something in the morning, sir, when
the papers come out. We could just be in luck. But there
doesn't seem a lot more we can do tonight.'

'Then I'll see you in the morning at nine.'

'If you need somewhere to doss, sir ...'

Gently shook his head. For him, the absence of local
accommodation presented no problem: just eight miles

further on, in the village of Welbourne, lay his own beloved Heatherings.

'Then fingers crossed, sir.'

'Fingers crossed.'

Automatically he chose the coast road, slowing as he approached the now-deserted coach, at this hour merely a dark shadow against the night of the marshes. A memory from Thorpe's childhood, situated beside a narrow byroad ... overlooked by none except the occasional fisherman visiting the little net store down on the beach. Who else could have known of its occupation, or guessed at the prize that waited there? Well, besides Dyball there was Christine Ford. Unless one or other of them had dropped a careless hint ...

Gently shrugged to himself – perhaps tomorrow. He drove on towards the sparkling lights of Holmeness. From higher up the coast came the flashes of a lighthouse, while out at sea a bobbing glimmer marked a fishing boat.

'It's for you, sir, a Mr Beamish.'

The morning had brought a fine day. Sun was warming the lawn at Heatherings and the purple acres that stretched beyond.

Overnight he had managed to contact Rouen and a sleepy sounding Gabrielle: 'You are at home, hah? You lucky policeman! And me, I am still stuck at Mont St Aignan ...'

His sleep had been fitful and he had woken bleary-eyed to receive his cup of tea from Mrs Jarvis. Now he rose with a sigh from the breakfast table and went through to the hall to pick up the phone. 'Any news?'

'Not exactly, sir. But I thought you would like to be kept in touch. We've had a ring from that Mr Hastings, the bloke whose wife chummie strangled.'

Gently grunted. 'So what's with him?'

'Not very much, sir, if you put it like that. His secretary

rang to give him the picture and like she told him she couldn't swear that the corpse was Thorpe's.'

'I trust you sorted him out.'

'I tried, sir. Then he asked if he couldn't talk to you. But I thought there was no call for that, so I told him you weren't available.'

'And – nothing else?'

'Just negative reports, sir.'

'Dyball?'

'Got legless and slept in the shelter.'

'No sightings of Thorpe with other people?'

'Afraid not, sir.'

'Thank you, Beamish.' He hung up with another sigh – no progress in the hours of darkness. Clearly some luck was going to be needed if they were to make ground with this case. Unless the money was tracked down or some suspicious contact revealed, they would be left holding thin air. And luck didn't seem to be coming their way . . .

'Will you be in to lunch, Mr Gently?'

Grumpily, before leaving, he strolled down the lawn to gaze at the heather; then smoked a pipe and glanced over the newspapers before going to his car.

'They've done us proud, sir.' Beamish, too, had been absorbing the morning's press. THE SLAYER SLAIN was the caption in the local, which also carried a shot of them with the coach in the background.

'Any results?'

'It's a bit early, sir, but we have had a call or two – people who've seen him near the coach, or doing his shopping here in the town.'

'But – always alone.'

'Except one caller, who did see him talking to Dyball.'

'Dyball we know about.'

'All the same, sir.'

'At the moment Dyball is a dead end.'

The phone rang. Beamish snatched it up eagerly, but then his eagerness visibly faded. 'No miss . . . I'm sorry

39

miss ... no, there's nothing fresh we can tell you.' He slammed the phone home.

'Miss Ford?'

Beamish nodded, his hand still on the instrument. 'I don't know, sir,' he said. 'That female gets at me somehow, the way she lays it on. I feel sure there's a connection somewhere. And the way she hesitated before coming to us – if she had come straight away, none of this might have happened.'

Reluctantly Gently shook his head. 'Her explanation is plausible. She was simply unsure of her identification.'

'But if she was an ex of his, sir, and found she had him over a barrel?'

'Still ... what then?'

'It could have been deliberate, her hanging on and not reporting him. She could have had some naughty ideas and him in no position to refuse her.'

But again Gently shook his head. 'You're forgetting she consulted with her boss and her friend. Everything supports the account she has given us. And the ordeal she was put through explains her concern.'

'Well ... if you say so, sir. But I still think there's a little more to it.'

'If there were it can be of no assistance to us.'

Beamish pulled a face. 'I suppose you're right, sir.'

But so it was. No amount of imagination could link Miss Ford with the violence at the coach. If indeed she had once been Thorpe's girl-friend then only her hesitation to shop him might be explained, and possibly her present state of distress. No more could be deduced from it than that.

'So, like it or not, we're left with Dyball, sir. And him you don't seem to fancy either.'

Gently shrugged. 'I'm told he was drunk last night. And it probably wouldn't have been the first occasion.'

Beamish was silent for a moment. 'You think he could have shot his mouth off, sir?'

'It isn't impossible.'

'Like where his dough came from – and where he could lay hands on plenty more?'

Gently nodded. 'He swears he didn't. And while he was sober that might have been true. But the odds are he was spending the money on drink and then caution may have gone out of the window.'

'Like he began boasting about it, sir.'

'His being in funds would attract attention. For a single session it might have escaped notice, but not when it became a regular thing. People would begin to ask questions and perhaps rib him about his sudden wealth. And the curious may have kept an eye on him and spotted where that sudden wealth was coming from.'

'They spotted Thorpe, sir . . .'

'They spotted him. And perhaps soon began to grasp the situation. Who he was they didn't need to know, just that he was a fugitive flush with loot.' Gently paused. 'It may be a mere supposition, but at the moment those are all we have. Somehow, the killer got to know of the money. And this may have been the way it happened.'

'You're damned right, sir.' Beamish's eyes glinted. 'And I should have thought of that myself.'

'So . . . a few questions asked round the pubs?'

'I'll put a couple of my best men on it.'

Orders were given. Gently lit a pipe and went to stare through the window at the busy street. His eye fell on a car that seemed vaguely familiar: a highly polished vermilion Mondeo. Slowly it was negotiating the traffic, as though in search of some unfamiliar destination, then finally it identified the police station, pulled over and double-parked.

Gently blew a smoke ring. 'We have a visitor.'

'Sir . . .?'

Beamish also came to stare. 'Do you know him, sir?'

Gently nodded. The man locking the car was Oswald Hastings.

*

41

'My business here was really with Christine, but I thought it best if I put in an appearance. I mean, if there is any way I can help, I shall be only too happy to oblige.'

Briskly he entered the office, holding out a hand first to Gently, then to Beamish: a city type, dressed in a pin-stripe suit, bow-tie, stylish brogues. 'You can appreciate how deeply this affects me, a tragedy like this so soon after the other. I found it difficult to credit when Christine rang me and she seemed uncertain about it herself. I suppose . . .?'

'There is no question, Mr Hastings.'

'If you should – if you require confirmation?'

'That will not be necessary.'

'I felt I should offer, though I must admit my relief that I won't have to do it. I have just come from talking to the poor girl and seen the effect it has had on her.'

'Regrettably, we needed her assistance.'

'Of course, I understand that. But I trust you won't need to come back to her. I doubt if Christine can take much more.'

Slowly, Gently nodded. 'She would have been a long-time acquaintance of Thorpe's?'

'Four years, that was how long he worked for us. She had contact with him every day.'

'They were closely acquainted?'

'In the office. Yes.'

'No more than that?'

Hastings stared. 'If you mean what I think you mean, then you can forget ideas of that sort. Thorpe wasn't her type and she wasn't his.' His mouth twisted. 'We know now what his was.'

'They had never been lovers?'

'Good God, no. Just seeing what she saw is what is upsetting Christine.' He stared away, then back at Gently. 'Dare I ask how close you are to an arrest? I believe, from the way I'm tied up with all this, that I have some right to know what is going on.'

Gently shrugged. 'The enquiry is proceeding.'

'Meaning?'

'We are taking every step to find the culprit.'

Hastings frowned. 'In other words?'

Gently struck a fresh light for his pipe. He said: 'Perhaps you should know one thing. The money that Thorpe took from your safe has not so far been recovered. When it is, you will be advised. But for the moment we have found no trace of it.'

The brown eyes bored into his. 'In short, you are alleging that theft was the motive?'

'It would seem likely.'

'That, for those few pounds!'

'The amount may not appear so modest to everyone.'

'It seems incredible.' Hastings shook his head. 'But I suppose you could be right. If this had happened back in town, nobody there would have raised an eyebrow. So – find the money and you've found your man. That's the way the cookie crumbles.'

Gently said nothing.

Hastings frowned for a moment. He said: 'And yet, from the way that Christine was telling it . . . I mean, the injuries that Thorpe received. If the motive was theft they seemed exorbitant.'

'We shall bear the injuries in mind.'

'They look like something . . . well, other. As though the theft was an afterthought, perhaps even intended to mislead.'

Gently regarded him. 'You have reason to think so?'

'Reason . . . no.' Hastings looked uncomfortable. 'But one can't help remembering – there was a certain person, one who wasn't too careful what he said to the press.'

'You refer to your brother-in-law?'

'Yvonne's brother, yes. I realise I shouldn't be bringing him up. But when Christine described what had happened to Thorpe, it was Norton who came into my mind. They were very close, he and Yvonne. Her death hit him hard. And the way he talked to the reporters . . . well, you must understand what I mean.'

Gently nodded. 'Thank you, Mr Hastings.'

'Forgive me if I'm trying to tell you your business. I'm a fool and you are probably right theft was the motive for the crime.'

'You may rely on us to take everything into account.'

'Of course. And I'm merely taking up your time. But since I was here . . .' He paused. 'I suppose I mustn't ask again if an arrest is expected?'

'You may ask.'

'Then – ?'

Gently shrugged.

'Understood,' Hastings said. 'So I'll leave you to get on with it and wish you success in your endeavours. If I'm needed, you know where to find me.'

He thought of offering his hand again, but didn't; and moments later the red Mondeo pulled away.


'Sir, I'm not quite up with this.'

Gently had lit a fresh pipe and was still staring through the window. It wasn't a new angle that Hastings had suggested, but one that had seemed too remote and improbable. Did Hastings know something, that he had brought it up – something he preferred to leave Gently to dig out? Ostensibly, his visit there that morning had been to offer assistance in confirming the identity of the body . . .

'This brother, sir – is he in the picture?'

If so, it was on the very edge.

'He made some threats when his sister's body was discovered. About what he would do if he caught up with Thorpe.'

'Threats like – doing for him?'

Gently puffed a few times. 'Norton was in a very emotional state. He said things that no doubt he has since regretted, but which the reporters made the most of.'

'Suppose he tracked him down, sir?'

'Then he was cleverer than we were.'

'It might explain the way Thorpe was knocked about . . .'

'It might. If he found him.'

44

'Perhaps that secretary . . .'

Gently blew a smoke ring and let it die. In the London investigation there had been no suggestion of a contact between Miss Ford and the victim's brother, and no likelihood, on the present occasion, of her passing information to him. But . . . then he paused, in the act of blowing a fresh ring. She had passed that information to Hastings: Hastings, who would have it in his power to relay it to a certain emotional firebrand . . . Could that be what Hastings was holding back on, when he introduced the Norton angle? Possible, but barely probable. Hastings, like himself, had perhaps merely remembered those threats . . .

'We'll bear Norton in mind, but for the moment concentrate on trying to locate the money. If we draw a blank on that it will be time to start checking the less likely angles.'

'Just thought it fitted so well, sir. And the money, it could be like the man said, chummie made off with it to fool us.'

'So we'll bear that in mind too. But meanwhile carry on with routine.'

'Right you are, sir.' Beamish sighed. 'You know these people better than we do.'

Weary of the office, Gently knocked out his pipe and sought the relief of the busy streets. On the promenade the first thing to catch his eye was Dyball, lounging in the shelter by the lifeboat, a couple of beercans beside him and a cigarette in his mouth. The down-and-out's eyes were carefully averted and appeared to be intent on the sea horizon. As Gently passed by he took a swig from a can, but never let his gaze drift from the water.

Nearby, one of Beamish's men leaned boredly against the railings.

'Any luck?'

The man shrugged. 'Around eight o'clock he went for a pee. Then he fetched beer and sandwiches from the supermarket, and came back here to eat his breakfast. Afterwards he went for a crap in the toilets and he hasn't shifted from here since.'

'Has anyone spoken to him?'

'No one.'

'He hasn't tried to make a touch?'

The man shook his head.

So the down-and-out was still in funds. Though by now he must be running it close.

'Keep a sharp eye on him.'

'Don't you worry, sir. I even followed him when he went for his pee.'

Gently strolled on. Luck was what they needed, but till now luck seemed to be passing them by – their only smell of it had been when the fisherman had volunteered his sighting of Dyball with Thorpe.

At the end of the promenade he continued towards the coach and the hut on the beach. Both were now deserted, the former locked and sealed, the latter surrounded by gulls, who rose, scolding at his approach. If only . . .

He advanced to the hut, the door of which he found unlocked. Inside, piles of folded nets; outside, nets hung out to dry between a line of posts. There were also a winch, launch-planks and frames, evidence that at times a boat was beached there; but Beamish had pursued his enquiries with the fishermen and found none who had been present at the critical time. And if not fishermen, then who else, at that lonely spot and at such an hour? He shook his head. Unobserved by any witness, the killer had gone about his deadly business . . .

He crossed the beach and the road to the coach, around which the guardian tapes still fluttered, and stood a while observing the scene in case some spark of inspiration still lingered there. None did. Even at this hour traffic was light on the road, strollers on the beach distant, yesterday's gapers gone about their affairs . . . He lit a pipe and smoked it, then finally set off back towards the town. They needed luck. Luck! Without it, the case was drifting towards the files.

*

46

'Sir, I think you should talk to Christine. If you have a moment, I'll fetch her down.'

It had been time for a drink and, after due consideration, Gently had chosen the bar at the White Hart.

'A pint of Adnam's . . .'

He had taken it to a seat by the window and had barely drunk the froth from it when Madge, Miss Ford's girl-friend, had hurried across to him.

'She wishes to speak to me?'

'No . . . but I think it's necessary. I expect you know her boss called in here this morning. They had a private conversation in our room and I found her in tears after he left. I asked her what had happened, but she wouldn't tell me, just that there was a decision she had to take. Then I caught sight of you from our window, coming over here, and made an excuse to leave her.'

Gently drank. 'And you have no idea?'

'No – but it must have been something he said.'

'Touching this business?'

'What else? She hasn't been herself again since it happened.'

Gently ghosted a shrug. 'Do you know Miss Ford well?'

'Of course. She's my best friend. We were at college together and it was Christine who got me my job at the agency.' She paused. 'Why do you ask?'

'Just a passing thought. Was there ever a connection between your friend and Thorpe?'

'With Jason? Never.'

'You can be certain?'

'Yes – as certain as I am standing here.' She blushed and looked away. 'If you had said someone else . . . but that has nothing to do with this business.'

'Someone – else?'

She nodded reluctantly. 'I suppose . . . well, it isn't a secret. Everyone knows. About men and their secretaries. You had only to ask at the office.'

'She – and Hastings?'

'Oswald. Yes.'

'She is his mistress?'

'I didn't say that. Just that as far as Christine is concerned there is only one man and that man is Ossie. For his part, I doubt if he cares two pins. She is merely his worshipping and terribly efficient secretary.'

'And . . . in some way, he has just upset her?'

She nodded. 'Yes. And I'm sure . . .'

'Leaving her with a decision to take.'

'Why do you think I came after you?'

Gently drank. 'Very well, then.'

'I'll bring her down to the private lounge. It's usually empty at this time of day. And perhaps you can order us a couple of coffees.'

She hurried off. Gently emptied his glass, gave the order and went through to the private lounge, which, it happened, had windows that looked up the coast in the direction of the old coach. Fortunately, he had asked that the serving of the coffees should be delayed, since it was a quarter of an hour later when the two ladies appeared. Supported on her friend's arm, the woeful-looking Miss Ford was guided across the lounge to where he was sitting.

'Really Madge, I don't know . . .'

'Hang on, Chrissie – they're bringing us coffee.'

The coffee was served. Miss Ford barely touched hers, sat staring helplessly at the cup.

At last Madge said firmly: 'Chris, you've nothing to be afraid of. If there's something you should tell the Superintendent, then it's best to get it off your chest.'

'But Madge, you can't know. I could be doing wrong . . .'

'You must leave him to decide about that.'

'It could make trouble for someone who . . .'

'Chris, the Superintendent is no fool.'

Desperately, Miss Ford applied herself to her cup. She was looking a mess, her blonde locks untended, her pallid features innocent of make-up. Never since she had entered the room had her eyes rested on Gently.

Gently said: 'This morning you learned something, Miss Ford?'

48

'No, no. It isn't like that.'

'In your conversation with Mr Hastings?'

'No, please. It isn't that at all.'

'Then . . .?'

'I – I don't know!'

'Yet something is troubling you?'

She choked down a sob. 'I could be doing wrong, I don't know. Oswald seemed to think . . . but if I tell you. And I'm so sure . . .'

'Sure of what, Miss Ford?'

She lapsed into tears.

'Chris, don't be an idiot,' her friend broke in. 'If you know something Oswald thinks you should tell the police, then tell them you should and no more nonsense.'

'But you don't know, Madge – I never told you. And I shouldn't have mentioned it to Os . . .'

'Chris, really!'

'Oh, how I wish we had never come to this place.'

She turned her face away and stared down the room. Madge glanced at Gently and made a helpless gesture. Miss Ford grabbed her cup and swallowed some coffee. Then she swung back to stare tremblingly at Gently. 'Very well, then – if you must – '

'Take your time, Miss Ford,' Gently said.

'Yes . . .' She drank more coffee. 'It was yesterday. Madge will tell you . . .'

'Yesterday?'

She nodded. 'I . . . I was feeling out of sorts. In the evening, after I'd spoken to you. Madge persuaded me to go for a stroll.'

'A stroll along the promenade,' Madge said. 'Then along the track to the Martello Tower. Most people were at the concert, so we had it pretty well to ourselves.'

'Pretty well . . . but down at the tower . . .?'

'You mean that fellow sitting in the marrams?'

'Yes, him.'

'Well, he looked harmless enough, just sat there staring at the breakers. Why should he upset you?'

'Because – because – ' She gulped coffee. 'I think he was someone I'd met before, when the investigation was going on in town. Someone who was involved . . .'

'Nonsense, Chris!'

'I'm almost certain.'

'After what you've been through you've started imagining things.'

'Madge, no! It was because I felt so certain that I mentioned it to Os this morning. And if it was him, I don't know ... most likely it could only have been a coincidence . . .'

Madge stared. 'So who is he supposed to be?'

Miss Ford stared into her empty cup. 'The brother,' she said. 'Ossie's wife's brother. Who said all those terrible things to the press. I can't remember his name, but it was him sitting there, staring at the sea.'

'Holy . . . Moses! And you're guessing he did it?'

Miss Ford wrestled with her cup and said nothing.

'But maybe it wasn't him,' Madge said. 'You can't be positive.'

And for some reason Miss Ford was sobbing again.

## 4

'Check the hotels and guest-houses. If Norton really was here we need to talk to him.'

On returning to the office, Gently's first move had been to ring the Yard. Information followed: Norton certainly wasn't in town, but absent on a fortnight's vacation, present whereabouts uncertain. He and his wife, who also worked at the Chelsea agency, had left town the previous weekend. She, it was thought, intended to visit her mother, but it was not known whether Norton was accompanying her. And the mother's address? Sorry, they didn't have it, only that she lived on the south coast somewhere.

'Now we know why Hastings brought his name up, sir.'

And perhaps why he hadn't been more specific. Once more, it rested with the hesitant Miss Ford, who might or might not not have reliable testimony . . .

The stroke of luck they needed? Well, perhaps. Grumpily, Gently drank coffee and fiddled with his pipe. Somehow, Norton didn't quite sink in with him, seemed still a marginal factor in the case. The business with the money . . . would it really have occurred to him, at that savage moment as he stood over Thorpe? Would he have dared waste time searching for it after such a deed, with every moment vital? And, finally, would he still be hanging about in Shinglebourne, risking recognition and investigation?

Either robbery was the motive for the crime or it had been a cold-bloodedly planned act of revenge, and Norton seemed to fit neither, rather to fall between the two.

'Did you ever meet him in London, sir?'

Gently shook his head. 'I sent a man to have a word with him. I think he was ashamed of his outburst to the press and he certainly didn't repeat it.'

'It's still a bit odd, sir, him being around here, with his

wife gone off somewhere else. Like he did have information from someone, whoever it might have been.'

'Like Miss Ford, he may have come here for the Festival.'

'I still think it strange, sir.'

'Or he may at this moment be in Bournemouth or Eastbourne.'

'If he has any sense, he's cleared out by now.'

The problem, however, was solved almost effortlessly by an agitated voice on the phone: Mrs Norton, ringing from Bognor, following a call from a colleague in Chelsea.

'You're looking for Christopher, Sheila tells me – I rang Scotland Yard and they told me to ring you. But surely you can't be thinking – I mean, it just isn't on!'

'We wish to speak to him, Mrs Norton.'

'Yes, but just because . . . It's unbelievable. And in any case there's nothing he can tell you, I had a long talk with him on the phone last night . . .'

'You know where he is?'

'I'm surprised you have to ask me.'

'Still . . .?'

'He's right there under your nose, room thirty-three at the Sea View Hotel.'

'Thank you, Mrs Norton.'

'But honestly . . .'

Gently replaced the phone.

'A couple of men, sir?' Beamish said.

Gently shrugged. 'Just the one.'

Half an hour later Christopher Norton was shown into the office, a tallish, well-dressed man of around forty, with bushy dark hair and alert grey eyes. He gave each of them a quick look before advancing to the chair placed for him, with a hard stare for the WPC who sat with her pad at one end of the desk.

'Please sit, Mr Norton.'

He took his seat.

'Now, as I am sure you will understand, we are investigating a crime that took place here yesterday, the death of a certain person suspected of one that occurred earlier. A man known to you, whom you may have recognised if you encountered him during your stay here. Wasn't it on Saturday that you arrived?'

His expression was a sneer. 'Didn't the hotel tell you that?'

'You had come for the Festival?'

'Oddly enough, that was my reason for being here.'

'So you have been present in the town since Saturday, attending concerts, mingling with the other visitors. In a situation where it is possible that you might have encountered this man.'

'If you say so.'

'Can you deny it?'

'Oh, far be it from me. And I'm the one who swore to wring his neck if ever I should clap eyes on him. Isn't that why I'm sitting here?'

'You admit to making such threats?'

'You've got them in black and white, haven't you?'

'Those threats were serious?'

'At the time, bloody serious. Hadn't that skunk just murdered my sister?' Norton glared at Gently. 'Wouldn't you have made them, if Yvonne had been a sister of yours – a sister whom he'd just got pregnant and who was daft enough to think he cared?'

Gently stared back. 'But now you're saying they're not serious.'

'I'm saying – no, now I've got more sense. I don't say I wouldn't have beaten the sod up, but then I would have handed him over to you. Is that good enough?'

Gently shook his head.

'Anyway, it's all sodding academic. I didn't run across him and it was someone else who gave the bastard what he deserved.'

'You deny meeting Jason Thorpe?'

Norton merely glared.

'And – at no time – were you in the neighbourhood of the place where he was hiding out?'

'I've seen it of course, who hasn't? If you drive out that way you can't miss it.'

'But you were never nearer to it than that?'

'No. Never.'

'Perhaps on a stroll along the beach?'

Was there a flicker in the staring grey eyes? If so, it had come and gone in an instant.

'Well?'

'No – I've never been that way. The Sea View is at the other end of the town, and I take my walks down towards the boats and the old tower.'

'You saw the coach merely when driving past it?'

'Yes. Just once, on my way to Thwaite.'

Gently paused, then nodded. 'Very well, Mr Norton. Now perhaps we can come to yesterday. If you will, I would like you to give me an account of your movements yesterday morning.'

His stare was bitter. 'And I know what that means. But you'll soon find that you're wasting your time. I was in Thwaite all day yesterday, for the Wagner concert at The Maltings. Ask Geoffrey Davis at the Sea View. He was with me and gave me a lift back.'

'You were there . . . all day?'

'Yes, all day. Oh, I know the concert didn't begin till after lunch, but I fancied a hike across the marshes and left my car at the hotel. Then I met Geoffrey for lunch at The Maltings and we went to the concert, which ended at six. And it wasn't until I got back here that I heard what had happened.'

'You . . . hiked to Thwaite across the marshes?'

'Yes, was there any harm in that?'

'Setting out at what time, Mr Norton?'

'Nine – perhaps later. I can't be certain of that.'

'And taking which route?'

'I don't know. It follows the course of the river . . .'

'The Sailor's Path, sir,' Beamish put in. 'That would have to be the one. And it starts off a few yards past the White Hart.'

'A few yards . . .?'

'That's right, sir. Just a stone's throw from you know what.'

'From the coach?'

'From the coach, sir.'

Norton stared at Beamish as though he could kill him.

'If you think for one moment . . .' Norton had jerked up straight on his chair, his hands working, a flush in his not unhandsome features.

'Calm yourself, Mr Norton.'

'But if you're trying to hang this thing on me . . .'

'We are pursuing an investigation.'

'Yes – and I don't like the way it's going.'

'That is regrettable. But we have a duty. It appears you were near the coach at a critical time. Perhaps, when you have calmed down, you can give us that time more precisely.'

'Perhaps – nothing!'

Gently shrugged. 'We have only to ask at your hotel. No doubt they will remember when you handed in your key.'

Norton gazed at him, his mouth quivering. 'You'd do that too, wouldn't you?' he said. 'You've got me where you want me. If I don't play ball, you'll put me inside.'

'If you will just answer the question.'

'I should ask for a lawyer.'

'That is permitted. If you feel it necessary.'

'Oh hell!' He twisted his hands. 'If you must know, I left the hotel some time before nine.'

'Some time . . .?'

'Nearer eight thirty, then. I was keen to be on my way. When you're stuck in town like I am you don't want to waste good opportunities.'

'So, by nine, or a little earlier . . .?'

He nodded. 'I was right there, where you want me. But that's all. I never went near the coach, never gave it a single frigging thought.'

'You saw no one in the vicinity?'

'Not a soul.'

'Nor met anyone?'

'No.'

'Possibly a vehicle on the road?'

He shook his head. 'Out to sea there was a fishing boat, but apart from that I was on my own.'

'A fishing boat . . .?'

'One of those long-shores, heading south down the coast. But the last person I saw was a waiter coming out of the White Hart.'

'And . . . you heard no suspicious sounds?'

Norton hesitated. 'Should I have done?'

Gently stared at him for a moment. He said: 'We have an estimated time of death for Thorpe. Your presence near the coach was within that period and may have coincided with the commission of the crime.'

'May have! Are you bloody saying – ?'

'Merely stating facts, Mr Norton.'

'What you're saying is I did for the bastard.'

'So far I am making no accusation.'

'So far. So bloody far.' He glowered at Gently, at the fascinated Beamish.

The WPC nervously selected a fresh pencil and made a little scribble on her pad.

Norton scowled at her. His mouth was tremulous. 'Listen,' he said. 'And write this down. I didn't do it, I didn't kill him, I didn't know the sod was within a thousand miles. Write that down.'

She glanced at Gently, then scribbled.

'And that's all I'm going to say.' Norton snarled. 'So now get on with it, do your darnedest, you're getting nothing more out of me.'

Gently shrugged. 'Perhaps a little co-operation – if you are as innocent as you declare?'

56

'*If* I am.'

'In your situation it might be the wisest response.'

Norton glared. 'You've had co-operation. And look where bloody co-operation has got me. No, thank you, no, sir. I'm not such a fool as you seem to think.'

'A little more I'm afraid we must insist on.'

'A little more . . .'

Gently nodded. 'In the circumstances we shall need to take your fingerprints and conduct a search of yourself and your room at the Sea View.'

'But – bloody hell!'

'You have an objection?'

Norton gazed wide-eyed. 'And if I have?'

'Then we must suppose you have something to hide and that we will not be wasting our time.'

'You . . . sod!'

'So?'

In answer, Norton jumped from his chair and, a moment later, was slamming the contents of his pockets on the desk in front of Gently.


In the end, the results were near enough negative. The jumble of objects could arouse little suspicion: a modestly well-furnished wallet accompanying a cheque-book in frequent use; then a fingerprint that might or might not have been a match for the smudge on the poker.

'Perhaps we'll have better luck at the hotel, sir.'

Norton's room was one that overlooked the beach, with a veranda, an *en-suite* bathroom and a miniature bar in one corner. In the wardrobe hung such an anorak as Norton might have worn on his trek across the marshes, along with a pair of jeans and, on a rack, a muddy pair of walking shoes. They went into a plastic sack. But of caches of banknotes there was no sign, though the search included Norton's car and an enquiry about any deposits in the hotel's safe.

'Could be he slung the dough, sir.'

Unfortunately, that was only too likely. The Chelsea estate agent was no Dyball to be dazzled into retaining possession of fatal loot. If he had taken it at all it was to mislead the inquiry, while scope to dispose of it had been at hand: the marshes, the river. Thrust into mud or sunk with a weight had been the probable fate of the twice-stolen money.

Unless Forensic could turn up something with the clothing, they had no grounds for pursuing Norton further.

'Satisfied now?'

His signed statement was waiting on the office desk. Gently glanced through it. It contained nothing that hadn't been elicited in the interrogation.

'We have just one further enquiry to complete.'

'A further enquiry . . .?'

Watching him closely, Gently explained. At first the expression in his eyes was uncomprehending, then it relaxed, becoming one of relief.

'You have no objection?'

'Good lord, no! You can test every stitch I brought with me. I'm asking you to. That way you'll have proof I'm not mixed up in this business.'

'A negative result would not be proof.'

'It'll be proof near enough.'

'Certain clothing could have been disposed of.'

Norton stared, but shook his head. 'Of course, you have to follow these things up and I don't blame you for being so thorough. But you must be getting the idea by now. I'm Yvonne's brother, but I'm not your man.'

Gently paused; nodded. 'And – you have no idea who he might have been?'

'Me?'

'With the involvement you remarked on.'

Norton simply stared a moment, then shook his head again. 'According to the papers some money was missing and that seemed to be the objectof the crime. If it wasn't, I can't help you. Nor can I if it was.'

58

'You are positive you saw no one at the scene of crime?'

'Yes.'

'Or, say, before? Or just after?'

'I mentioned the waiter – '

'A woman, perhaps?'

'A woman?' His stare was sharp. 'Is it – what's her name – Christine, we're talking about, the blonde secretary who hangs about Oswald?'

'You know her, then?'

'Of couse. Yvonne wasn't too happy about her. And she's here for the Festival, I've seen her around, but not at the place and time you're thinking of.' He hesitated. 'You can't seriously think – ?'

'Merely enquiring, Mr Norton.'

'Well, the answer is no, I didn't see her, nor anyone else at all.'

'Not at the scene? Not up the track?'

'I didn't see a soul between there and Thwaite. I'm sorry I can't be more helpful, but that's how it was, the way I've written it down.'

Gently sighed. 'Then that's all for the moment. You are free to leave, Mr Norton. I must require you to hold yourself available and that you remain in Shinglebourne until further notice. Is that understood?'

His head jerked. 'Understood.'

'Then you are free to go on your way.' He hesitated, frowning at Gently, but finally shrugged and made for the door.

Beamish watched his departure grimly. 'Do you want me to put a man on him, sir?'

Gently shook his head. 'I don't think that's necessary. But perhaps someone to check the dustbins at the Sea View.'

'In case he dumped some gear?'

'Just in case. Though I think Norton would be too intelligent. But we can't take chances, so put a man on it and get the other stuff off to Forensic.'

'Straight away, sir. I like this geezer – he's got the motive we're looking for. I never could quite see it as a robbery, the way someone took that poker to Thorpe.'

'So. No chances.' Gently brooded. 'And perhaps a few enquiries among the fishermen.'

'The fishermen . . . ?'

He nodded. 'According to Norton there was a long-shore boat close to, one that could have been launched from the beach that morning at a very interesting time. If so, we need to talk to whoever was in it, so do your best to turn him up.'

Beamish promised. Gently lit a pipe and sifted again through Norton's statement.


A step closer – or was it?

About Norton he found it hard to make his mind up. The man troubled him, on one count a hot prospect, on the other an unfortunate innocent. The facts were suggestive, but the man? In the end, Gently had found himself almost liking him, willing to accept the truth of his testimony and the innocence on which he insisted. And yet . . . Wasn't there something unspoken, some matter Norton was holding back on? Gently blew smoke rings. He had had that feeling. Perhaps, he hadn't asked Norton the right questions . . .

Ford. Christine Ford.

Had something been touched on there?

Christine Ford at the White Hart – which overlooked the scene, was almost on the doorstep.

Her bedroom or her bathroom might have faced in that direction and her curiosity about the coach was already aroused; while dressing, while engaged in her toilet, wouldn't her gaze have kept turning that way?

She had been reluctant to report her sighting of Thorpe and afterwards her sighting of Norton. Why? In the case of the latter, was there a little more that could have been told?

Norton setting out on his trek. But from a direction other than the town . . .

Yet if this had been so, what had prevented her from mentioning it, in those first emotional moments in the presence of the body?

And if there was an unavowed connection between them, why make up a story about spotting him later in the week and bringing Norton to their attention at all?

An unavowed connection . . . Gently shook his head. Too clearly, Norton had no time for her. While, if her friend were to be believed, Miss Ford had time only for her boss. It was him, not her friend, she had consulted and whose advice she had accepted with such woeful reluctance. And who had deftly prepared the way, with Gently, for the disclosure that he had advised . . .

So, no step forward. Unless Forensic could provide it.

He knocked out his pipe in Beamish's ashtray and quit the office for the street.


'Anything fresh?'

'He doesn't shift, sir. Nor I don't think he will while we've got an eye on him.'

It was lunch-time in Shinglebourne and the promenade was almost deserted.

Gently had taken his meal in a pub near the Moot Hall, deliberately avoiding the White Hart and Miss Ford – fresh cod and juicy chips, with a pint of Adnam's to keep it company. Now, pipe in mouth, he had sought the Front and, inevitably, the shelter by the lifeboat.

There, Dyball continued to sprawl among his beer cans and screwed-up paper bags, while Beamish's bored DC crouched by the railings, pretending to ignore him.

Was Dyball drunk? It was difficult to tell. He lounged, with glazed eyes fixed on the sea. Occasionally his hand would reach for a can, but the direction of his gaze never wavered.

61

Though Gently had passed within a couple of yards of him the eyes had never as much as flickered.

'Has he made any fresh purchases?'

'A bag of chips and a pie, sir, from the stall you can see. And he's been to the toilets a few times, like he might have got the runs. Other than that he just sits there. Of course, I could always move him on.'

Gently shook his head. 'When is your relief due?'

'At two, and I shan't be sorry to see him!'

'You can run along now.'

'Sir?'

'I'll take over here. You get along and have your lunch.'

The DC stared. 'Well . . . if it's all right, sir . . .'

'Call it an order,' Gently said.

A little doubtfully, the DC obeyed and Gently took his place by the railings. It was a few years now since his last stake-out, but this was only to be for another half-hour . . .

Had the down-and-out noticed?

Apparently not. He went on stubbornly gazing into space. But then – could it have been chance? – when Gently began to fill his pipe, Dyball reached into his pocket for a cigarette and was obliged to shift position a little, to turn his face for a moment towards Gently.

Gently ignored him, lit his pipe, swivelled to lean on the railings and watch the beach. From the corner of his eye he could still see the down-and-out, whose face was not fully turned towards him. Nervously, the cigarette was lit and, after a few puffs, a can was raised. Then, shakily, Dyball got to his feet and stretched himself, before sitting again, though in a more alert posture.

Something on his mind?

Gently made no move, continued staring idly at the beach. Children were playing with a ball on the tide line, a couple sun-bathed, two youths were swimming. Peacefully he watched them, drew leisurely puffs, seemed to have forgotten Dyball entirely. Perhaps? But Dyball wasn't taken in. He remained sitting stiffly among his beer cans . . .

Five minutes passed. Then. Further up the beach some other children were flying a kite. Now a few more strollers were seeking the promenade, keeping their eyes firmly averted from the layabout in the shelter. One alone paused to stare, an elderly gentleman, who frowned and made a motion to his pocket; but then shrugged and walked on. Perhaps it was the beer cans that put him off?

A cleaner in overalls arrived at the toilet, pushing a trolley loaded with gear. He, too, stared at Dyball before collecting a bucket and disappearing inside.

And Dyball was staring back – intently. Was there a connection between those two . . .?

The cleaner was a rugged-looking fellow and his stare at Dyball had been almost threatening . . .

More time passed. One could hear the man at work and at last he emerged again with his bucket. But he merely shoved it back on the trolley and trundled off without a further scowl towards Dyball.

A glance – a quick glance – towards Gently.

Gently was absorbed in the dancing kite.

A moment, then Dyball was on his feet and slinking quickly across to the toilet.

Another dose of the runs that the DC had mentioned?

Gently turned to lean his back on the railings. One minute, two, three. Then the down-and-out reappeared.

He looked towards Gently, he couldn't help it, but succeeded in avoiding his eye and slunk, almost crept, back to the shelter to resume his sprawl and his empty gaze.

Had a need for a pee been all that was at the bottom of it?

Gently knocked out his pipe on the railings. He dealt Dyball a hard stare as he passed him and went directly into the toilet, which was still damp from the cleaner's ministrations.

It was small: a urinal and two WCs. Also ancient. The WCs were of the pattern with overhead cisterns and dangling chains. Two cisterns, two chains . . . and one chain slightly swinging. In a moment Gently had climbed on the seat. On top of the cistern nothing, but jammed in behind it . . . between cistern and wall . . .

He was down again in a flash and through the door into the street. But he was too late.

The only sign, now, of Dyball was the collection of empty beer cans and screwed-up paper bags.

## 5

'There can't be much doubt now, sir. His little dabs are all over them.'

Gently sat, furious with himself, staring at the objects lying on the desk. He needed only to have waited. A few minutes later the relief man had arrived on the scene and Dyball could have been under surveillance while Gently made his search of the toilet. Instead . . . He had scanned the promenade, belted through an alley that connected with the back street, thrust open the door of the nearest pub, but to no purpose: the down-and-out had escaped him. If Gently had read Dyball's mind, then Dyball had certainly read Gently's . . .

'There's still three thousand odd in the envelope, sir, and another hundred in the wallet.'

Also the wrist-watch, a gold Longines, along with a cheque-book and credit cards. All stashed away behind the cistern where Dyball could keep a ready eye on them. And from where, behind the bolted door of the compartment, he could safely abstract a note when he needed it . . .

He could not have gone far. The hunt had begun almost directly. And unless he had taken advantage of that last sally, the odds were that he was low on cash. If he had vanished it was to a hide-out in the town, from which hunger must at last drive him. In hours, at most days, he would come to hand . . . but he could have been sitting in a cell at that moment.

'I've sent Bidwell to the boat-yards, sir, and Stubbs is checking out the old warehouse. Then there's the coal yard and stables. Fowler is going to attend to them.'

'Has Dyball any friends here who might hide him?'

'Not him. He's always been a loner.'

'He had a chance to grab a handful of cash.'

'I can't see him hiring a taxi, sir.'

'Then keep an eye on vacant properties. There must be some, even with the Festival on.'

'I warned the men. But like you say, sir, there won't be many at this time of year.'

To rub it in there was a call from Forensic, who could find nothing suspicious about the garments submitted to them, while Bidwell had long since been relieved of the chore of searching through the Sea View dustbins.

Meanwhile patrol cars covered the two routes out of town, and departing yachts and fishing boats were under scrutiny . . .

'It's just a question of time, sir.'

Only it needn't have been. Savagely, Gently chewed on an unlit pipe. And . . . worse was to come.

The desk man entered. 'There's a man who wants a word with you, sir. Name of Hopkins, looks like a fisherman. Says it's to do with what happened at the old coach.'

'So send him in.'

A man in his forties, clad in the regular slop and jeans, he came in looking a little apologetic, carrying his cap in his hand. 'I'm sorry – I would have been here sooner, but I've only just got back. Then they told me what had happened and that you'd been asking after me . . .'

Gently gazed at him. 'Was it you who set sail yesterday morning from near the old coach?'

'Yes . . . but I didn't know. I spent last night down at Harford, where it was easier to drop my catch. My brother lives there . . .'

'At what time yesterday did you leave?'

'At half past seven. To catch the tide.'

'But you would have been there earlier?'

'Yes, of course. To load my nets and winch her down.'

'And you saw something?'

'Well . . . yes. But I didn't know then it was anything special. It was only when I got back here that I heard you'd been asking after me . . .'

66

'So what did you see?'

He gulped. 'This fellow. I don't know his name . . .'

'Can you describe him?'

'An old bloke with a beard, who lives rough round here. I've often seen him by the coach, I think it likely he dosses there. It could be I woke him up when I started with the winch.'

'You saw him leaving the coach?'

'I saw him come out. He was shoving something into his pocket. He gave a look in my direction, then went off towards the town.'

'Did you see what it was he put in his pocket?'

'No, how could I? A bit bulky it was, like a package or something. But that's all. He cleared off and I went on launching *Mary Jane*.'

'You had heard nothing earlier?'

He frowned. 'Should I have done?'

'I'm asking you.'

He shook his head. 'Down there the only thing you can hear is the surf. This bloke wasn't shot, was he?'

Gently gave him a stare.

'I didn't know,' Hopkins said. 'It wasn't till I got back just now. Last night we just sat yarning and I left this morning before the papers.' He hesitated. 'Have you got the old bloke?'

'Thank you,' Gently said, 'Mr Hopkins. You have given us useful information and now we require a written state-ment from you.'

'Yes . . . well.'

He looked somehow disappointed. Beamish led him out of the office. And Gently chewed his pipe some more and scowled at the gear lying on the desk.


So, a question of time . . . though was it really so simple?

When the phone rang Gently almost ignored it. And, when he found the caller was Madge, almost slammed it down again.

'Listen ... Christine doesn't know I'm ringing, but after the way he carried on ...'

'Are we still talking about Mr Hastings?'

'For heaven's sake, no! I'm talking about the brother.'

'Christopher Norton?'

'Yes, her brother. He came here after you had been questioning him. And he was swearing at Chrissie for reporting him to you and just about everything else. That man is dangerous.'

'What else was he blaming her for?'

'Well, I'm not sure I should repeat this. It seems that Mr Hastings isn't able to have children and didn't tell Yvonne until after they were married. And Chrissie should have spoken up, because she knew, because that was why Ossie's first wife divorced him. Instead, she kept quiet and Yvonne took a lover, and so Chrissie was responsible for that too.'

'He actually blamed her for that?'

'Yes. And for putting you on to him. I tell you, he's dangerous and if I hadn't been there I don't know what he might have done.'

'Mr Norton is apt to be outspoken.'

'He's dangerous and he's really got it in for Chrissie. I know he's cleared out now, but I felt that you should be told.'

Gently paused. 'He has cleared out?'

'Slung out is probably more like it. After you made enquiries at the Sea View they would be keen to see the back of him.'

'And you know this for a fact?'

'I've just rung them. I was going to warn him to stay clear of Christine.'

'And ... he had left?'

'So they told me. And they didn't sound too unhappy.'

Gently shook his head. Did it matter any longer? 'I doubt if you need to worry, Miss – ?'

'The name is Simpson. And I do worry. I believe that man to be capable of anything.'

'As I said, he is apt to be outspoken, but his outbursts are usually short-lived. However, I will bear in mind what you have told me and speak to him if the occasion arises.'

'He could have done that job at the coach.'

Gently laid down the phone.

And yet . . .?

Frowningly, he reached for the phone book and sorted out the number of the hotel. 'Police. May I speak to the manager?'

It was much as Madge Simpson had imagined. When Norton had returned to the hotel it had been hinted to him that his presence there was no longer desirable. The hint had been superfluous. The decision had already been taken. He had packed his bags and it remained only for him to settle his account.

'Did he leave a forwarding address?'

'Not as such, sir. But we can give you his home address in Chelsea.'

'At what time did he leave?'

'He's only just gone, maybe half an hour ago.'

Gently shrugged. Doubtless the estate agent was on his way to join his wife in Bognor – a petty annoyance, when he'd been required to stay put, but probably little more than that. And in view of his harassment of Miss Ford, perhaps the best thing that could have happened.

'It was still a bit cheeky of him, sir.' – Beamish wasn't quite so happy with the development. 'I mean, he's a sus, he was there on the spot, he should have known better than to run off like that.'

'It would have been more sensible to have informed us.'

'We could put out a call, sir.'

'Ring his wife in Bognor and tell her to ask him to get in touch when he arrives.'

She was rung. She expressed surprise. Norton had not advised her of any change of plan and she was sure he meant to see the Festival out, especially the Wagner concerts at The Maltings. But, if he did turn up in Bognor she would certainly do what they requested . . .

Beamish shook his head as he hung up. 'You're probably right, sir. But it's still a bit thick.'

'Meanwhile, step up the hunt for Dyball.'

'You can depend on that, sir.'


'I don't think Henry has a patient with him, George, but I'll just go through and check.'

Bored with the office, Gently had elected to pay a call on his old acquaintance, Dr Capel. Capel it was who had been called out to the coach and who had supplied them with a TOD; an estimate almost identical to the one they had later received from Forensic.

The Festival was usually a busy time with him, though not necessarily in the office of his profession. As first violin in the Shinglebourne Quintet he had other concerns occupying his attention and, in fact, as Gently had noticed on a programme, was engaged that evening in a Mozart recital.

'It's all right – he's only filling in forms. I'll make some coffee and bring it in.'

Tanya, Capel's gay little wife, waved Gently to the door leading to the doctor's consulting room.

Tall and gaunt, Capel rose stiffly from the desk at which he had been sitting and held out a large hand.

'Professional or friendly?'

Gently grinned. 'It could be a bit of both, with you. But mostly the latter. We've reached the stage where we're waiting for routine to turn something up.'

'Something – or someone?'

Gently nodded. 'We may have this thing sorted out by tonight.'

'By tonight . . . then can I offer you a ticket?'

'I would say yes, but – ' Gently shrugged.

'Well, take a seat.'

Capel's consulting room was as much like a lounge as a place of business, with its easy chairs, framed prints, bookshelves and model yacht. Gently chose a chair by the french windows, looking out over the well-trimmed lawn and, after shuffling some forms in a folder, Capel took a chair opposite. He stared at the garden for a moment. 'A lousy business,' he said. 'I've been following it in the local press and still can't quite grasp how it happened. Are they right when they say money comes into it?'

Gently nodded. 'A substantial sum. Thorpe robbed the company safe before he fled, but we found no money with the body.'

'No question he was guilty of strangling that woman?'

'Her body was found on a bed in his flat.'

'Motive and opportunity?'

'Both. And he wasted no time in making himself scarce.'

'He came here . . .?'

'According to his sister, the place was familiar to them when they were children. Their parents attended the early Festival and they used to play around the old coach.'

'A safe place, he would think.'

'Yes. Only the Festival brought people here who could recognise him.'

Capel frowned. 'People?'

'By ill chance, a woman who worked with him. The secretary of the man whose wife was his victim and who reported Thorpe's presence to us. But just too late.'

Capel hesitated. 'You are not thinking . . .?'

Gently shook his head.

'She would have known about the money.'

'No. You saw the corpse. One can't suspect it of being the crime of a woman.'

Capel sighed. 'Of course, you're right. And you would have arrested her long since. But you mentioned "people". Is there someone else who might fit the bill better?'

'Perhaps.'

'But I don't get told?'

Gently shrugged. 'Call it professional confidence. We may know of a person with a degree of motive that has no connection with money. But money was taken. And the routine I spoke of is directed towards the money.'

Capel gazed at him. 'Then you've found it?'

71

Gently turned his attention to the lawn.

'And – the thief?'

Gently reached for his pipe and began to fill it.

'You old devil!' Capel said. 'But I suppose you're right, and I shouldn't be asking. Though if you're expecting to wrap this up tonight, and it involves the money, you can't blame me for putting two and two together.'

He also took out a pipe, filled and lit it, and for a while they sat smoking puff for puff. He was frowning, but before he could begin again they were interrupted by Tanya with the coffee.

'Two lumps, George? Are you staying in town?'

A spell of enquiries and exchanges followed: Gabrielle's return from Rouen, the progress of the Festival, Henry's problems with the Quintet . . .

Then, finally, after a glance from her husband, Tanya poured herself a second cup, smiled knowingly at Gently and tripped out.

Capel drank coffee and relit his pipe. 'I still can't figure it,' he said. 'Of course you know the ropes, George, none better. But the way that fellow was knocked about. One blow would have rendered him senseless, there should have been no need to finish him off.'

Gently nodded. 'It wasn't the crime of a professional.'

'You mean?'

'The perpetrator may have feared recognition.'

'Then . . . it was someone Thorpe would have known?'

Gently blew a smoke-ring.

'I see,' Capel said. 'But still theft was the motive?'

Gently shrugged. 'It was the crime of an amateur, a one-off. In that situation a perpetrator can lose his head and go too far. Unfortunately such things happen, especially if recognition is a possibility.'

Capel stared keenly. 'So . . . you do know your man.'

Was there any point in pretending otherwise? 'Before Thorpe arrived here the coach was occupied by a down-and-out, a character well known to the local police. We

72

have evidence that Thorpe bribed him to vacate the place and we've traced the missing money to him.'

'Great Scot! You don't mean old Dibble?'

'Dyball is the man's name.'

'And he did all that?'

'We have additional testimony: that he was seen emerging from the coach at the critical time. Do you know the man?'

'Know him! I've had him here doing jobs in the garden.'

'A man in his fifties, with a beard?'

'Yes, old Dibble. He's been around several years.'

'Unfortunately he was wise to us finding the money and disappeared before we could arrest him. Hence the routine I mentioned. A full-scale search for him is in progress.'

'Oh dear – poor Dibble.'

'Have you seen him lately?'

'Not since this business blew up.'

'If you do, I need hardly tell you that you have a duty to inform us.'

Capel shook his head. 'It's a shock,' he said. 'I'm finding it hard to take this in. I've known old Dibble a long while. He's a terrible liar, but that's the worst I know of him. Could he have been on the booze?'

Gently shrugged. 'It's possible.'

'I think he would have to have been.' Capel frowned. 'I've always found him such a mild-mannered old bloke, I just can't see him cutting loose with a poker. And you're sure of your facts?'

Gently blew smoke. 'So he did jobs in your garden?' he said.

'Just weeding and a bit of hedge clipping. And once I had him mow the lawn.'

'So the garden is familiar to him.'

Capel stared.

'And there is access to the kitchen garden, at the back?'

'You devil,' Capel said. 'Do you think I'm harbouring him?'

'Perhaps', Gently said, 'we should take a look.'

73

Tight-faced, Capel accompanied him down the lawn to the kitchen garden where, in the boundary hedge, a gate opened on a lane. The gate was bolted, but quite climbable. Nearby was a greenhouse and potting shed. Gently explored them. No Dyball. Nor in the shrubbery that bounded the lawn.

'If I didn't know you, George . . .' Capel said.

And, in the end, he was unconvinced. If it wasn't the crime of a woman, almost equally it wasn't the crime of a Dyball. Hadn't Gently hinted at another prospect, someone with a motive unconnected with the robbery – such a one as might better fit the mayhem they had encountered in the old coach?

It was a point, but Gently didn't pursue it.

With a bleak expression Capel saw him out.


Back at the office the news continued negative, though by now the search had gone on for two hours, time enough for every likely refuge in the little town to have received a visit. Derelict buildings, obscure yards, pubs, cafés, even the church, all had received attention, none had offered a trace of the fugitive. Nor had any sightings been reported. Dyball seemed to have vanished into thin air. The last contact with him had been Gently's when, so precipitately, he had dashed into that toilet . . .

'Do you reckon he could have thumbed a lift out of town, sir?'

To do that, he would need to have acted promptly. Only two roads led away from Shinglebourne and no time had been wasted in putting a watch on them.

'Has a man been down to the old tower?'

'Bidwell, sir. And from there you can see the track over the marrams.'

'The Sailor's Path?'

'We talked to a couple who had come that way from Thwaite.'

'And, just a possibility, the old coach?'

74

'Fowler thought of that one, sir. He checked it inside and out, and likewise the net store on the beach.'

Thin air . . .

Yet a refuge somewhere must be concealing the down-and-out, some familiar nook or cranny, which his ramblings had revealed to him. It could not have been far. The hunt was up too quickly. In minutes he must have been at his hide-out. First, a rapid retreat to evade Gently, then directly to that obscure sanctuary . . .

'The lifeboat. Has that been investigated?'

Beamish looked doubtful. 'Wouldn't have thought he'd have risked that, sir. He'd know they do a daily check on her.'

'Still, give her a look.'

'May as well, sir. We haven't had much luck elsewhere.'

'And double-check all that area: the promenade, the alleys, the street behind.'

'If you say so, sir.'

'The odds are he didn't waste time when he went to ground.'

The telephone rang. Beamish snatched it up. 'It's Mr Hastings, sir.'

Gently took it. 'Yes?'

'Ah, Superintendent. Miss Simpson has just rung to tell me the news about Yvonne's brother. I'm not too happy, Superintendent. Madge tells me his manner to Christine was threatening. I hesitate to say this, but in my experience of him Norton is a man with a temperament of violence. Have you arrested him yet?'

'You will excuse me, Mr Hastings . . .'

'Isn't it true that he tried to do a bunk?'

'Please rest assured . . .'

'I wish to know, Superintendent. It could be that my secretary needs your protection.'

'In that case she will receive it, Mr Hastings.'

'But have you found him? Is he under arrest?'

'Be assured that the matter has our attention and that any necessary steps will be taken.'

Hastings paused. 'And that is all you can tell me?'

'We may have further information later.'

'About Norton?'

'I must request your patience.'

There was a longer pause at the other end. 'Please understand, Superintendent, I don't wish to be unjust to my brother-in-law. But I have had a long experience of the man and find it hard to resist a certain conclusion. If the same conclusion has occurred to you, it can be no great surprise to me.'

'Thank you, Mr Hastings.'

'Also, with regard to Christine, he bears a quite unwarrantable grudge. Please do bear that in mind.'

'It will not be forgotten.'

'In that case . . .' The phone went dead.

Beamish stared as Gently hung up. 'Had those women been on to him, sir?'

'They've been on to him. In his view, Miss Ford requires our protection.'

'From Norton, sir?'

'From Norton. Who Hastings is convinced is the man we are after.'

'Little does he know, sir!'

'Perhaps.' Gently fingered the phone. 'Always, with Hastings, one gets the impression that he could say more if he had a mind to.'

'About Norton . . .?'

Gently stared.

'Like he's got that one on his brain, sir. And with him taking off too – he'd have had that from the ladies.'

'So . . . let's get on with checking the lifeboat.'

Beamish sighed. 'I suppose it's worth a try, sir.'


A crew member helped them unlace the tarpaulin, but the mere necessity for it told them all: no sanctuary-seeking fugitive could have refastened it from within. Their assistant also unlocked a hut containing equipment and delved behind a stack of cannisters, but the site was clean. Still the only tokens of Dyball were the beer cans strewn in the shelter.

'Perhaps he jumped in the sea and swam off to Holland, sir!'

But Gently wasn't in the mood for jesting. On that spot he had made the mistake that had permitted the down-and-out to elude them. The prom, shelter, toilets, looming lifeboat . . . the alley leading to the back street behind. And the beach. Could he have jumped down there, crouching out of sight in those first hectic moments? It wasn't impossible. He'd have to move fast. And then, when Gently had darted down the alley . . .

Gently went to the rail and stared down at the sand and pebbles below, where jumping feet might have left deep prints. Only . . . none had. Dyball had left no signature.

'I'd best get back, sir. Something may have come in.'

If there was an answer, didn't it have to be here? Left to himself, Gently strolled through the area, inspecting each building, each doorway, each yard. Then the shop on the prom.

'Would you know Samuel Dyball?'

'A man was in here earlier, asking about him . . .'

'Have you seen him since?'

'No, I told the bloke. He was in here at lunch-time. He bought some sandwiches and a couple of cans, but that's the last I've seen of him.'

Gently also bought a can and carried it with him back to the shelter. Like Dyball . . . After clearing the bench of its refuse, he sat down in the same place. There he had lingered, the down-and-out, aware of the detective's eye upon him, conscious of riches stashed in the toilet, suspicious of every customer who entered it. Yes, he'd had the runs. If any customer had tarried there, Dyball's bowels could be relied on to have troubled him. A quick check, then back to his beer cans and his innocent gaze at the sea horizon . . .

Gently untabbed the can and drank.

77

But then a crisis had begun to develop: the bored detective, waiting for his relief, had been replaced by the eagle-eyed boss-man.

And worse! At that precise moment his enemy, the toilet cleaner, had arrived, a man who, besides his regular duties, might at times run a wiper over the cisterns . . .

Boss-man or not, when the cleaner withdrew, a bout of the runs had to overtake Dyball. Trying to seem casual, he'd slunk over to the toilets, hitched up on a seat and run his hand behind the cistern. Safe. His fortune was safe. As casually, he'd crept back out of the toilets . . . but somehow, he'd caught the boss-man's eye and in a flash had realised that the game was over. Yes, the boss-man was heading for the toilets and it was too much to expect he would miss what was hidden there . . . time to go, go, go, or in minutes a hand would be on his shoulder.

So . . . go where?

A leap on to the beach?

But the promenaders would notice, would give him away.

The alley?

It led only to the street, which offered no instant refuge.

Then – then?

Gently quaffed beer.

Somewhere close, somewhere credible.

His eye came back to the toilets, plural. On one side the men's . . .

More beer! And none need have noticed – the ladies' was behind, the men's in front; one could slip past the latter and into the former in the shake of a lamb's tail. Wasn't it possible – was anything else possible? How, otherwise, could their man have vanished so completely . . .?

Annoyingly, at that moment, the promenaders were few, consisting mostly of men and children, with the only female a giggling teenager clinging to the arm of her boy-friend. He needed someone more responsible . . . He scanned the promenade in either direction and finally . . . yes! Emerging from the alley, trailing a Scottie-dog on a lead . . .

'Excuse me, madam.'

She stared at him dismissively, an elderly lady with wavy grey hair, dressed in a two-piece and a ruffled blouse on which was pinned a cameo brooch. 'You wanted something?'

'Police. I would be obliged to have your assistance.'

'You are not drunk by any chance?' – she gestured to the beer cans.

He ducked his head. 'If you will let me explain.'

It required the production of his police warrant, but at last she agreed to do what he was asking. Leaving him holding the Scottie's lead, she stalked primly into the ladies'. There was a pause. He heard her voice raised interrogatively. Then, as primly, she stalked out again.

'There is someone . . .?'

'Oh, yes. And the place is stinking of tobacco smoke.'

'Did the person speak to you?'

'The person did not. But I could hear his heavy breathing.'

'His . . .?'

'It is a man in there. I could see his feet, under the door. And I trust' – she stared hard at Gently – 'that he gets his just deserts for hiding in there.'

Gently nodded. 'We shall certainly deal with him.'

'And now, if you don't mind, I will be on my way.'

'Just one favour more. If you will call at the police station and ask them to send me assistance . . .'

He watched her depart, the Scottie trotting behind her, then returned to the shelter and his watch on the toilets.

# 6

'Better give him a meal and time to settle down.'

The arrest of Dyball had not been straightforward. Leaving Bidwell to guard the entry, he and Beamish had entered the toilet. The place did indeed reek of tobacco smoke. It was the second of the two doors that was bolted; and, without too much stooping, one could see two scuffed shoes through the aperture below it.

'Police, Dyball. Time to open up.'

No response from behind the door.

'Are you hearing me, Dyball? We've come to collect you.'

Just the heavy breathing that the lady had reported.

'Dyball, you've given us enough trouble . . .'

'Go away . . . I haven't finished . . .'

'God Almighty! Are we supposed to believe that?'

'There's one next door . . .'

'Give me patience!'

'Dyball,' Gently said. 'We shan't go away. There are some questions you have to answer. You will do best to give yourself up and not waste any more of our time.'

'No, I haven't finished . . .'

'It will be best.'

'But I tell you . . .'

'We may have to use force.'

There were scuffling noises behind the door, the clap of a dislodged seat-lid.

'Dyball?'

'Go away!'

'Let me get at that door, sir,' Beamish said. 'You can't talk to a wallie like him, a strong arm is all they understand.'

'You leave me alone!'

'Open this door.'

'No.'

'I'm coming in, Dyball.'

'But I haven't done anything – '

'Ha-ha.'

'No, I haven't.'

'Watch yourself, my man.'

Beamish launched himself at the door, accompanied by a squeal from within. But the door, a sturdy, old-fashioned example, wasn't giving in so easily. A second attempt was no more successful and ended in Beamish nursing a bruised shoulder.

'Bidwell – come in here.'

'Right you are, sir.'

Inside, Dyball was sobbing hysterically. 'Please . . . please . . .'

'Go for it, Bidwell.'

'No . . . please . . .'

'Go for it, Bidwell.'

Bidwell tried, but fared no better.

'Blast!' Beamish said. 'We'll have to get a ram – why did they build these sods like this?'

'Half a mo', sir, let's try it like this.' Bidwell lifted his foot and drove it at the door at bolt level. 'It's giving . . .'

Another try; and one more did the job. The door crashed open to reveal a terrified Dyball crouching above the seat of the toilet.

'Don't – don't – !'

'Down you get, my man.'

'Please – please – don't hurt me.'

'I should worry! Off that seat.'

'Oh, please . . .'

'Do I have to fetch you?'

Sobbing, trembling, the down-and-out slithered down from the seat, to be led outside to the waiting squad car. Once he made a move as though to run for it, but Bidwell's grasp was firm on his arm. In silence they drove back to the police station, where Dyball was disposed of in a cell.

'Phoo!' – Beamish nursed his shoulder. 'And to think we

searched the whole ruddy town for him. It's comic, sir, when you come to think of it, him all the time sitting there in the ladies' bog. What gave you the idea, sir?'

Gently shrugged. Hadn't it been his own guilt that had drawn him back to those toilets?

'Anyway we've got him, sir, and after he's sweated on it I don't think he'll give us a lot of trouble.'

Probably not. And there might even have been time for that concert, after all.

'Sit yourself, Dyball.'

It was two hours later when he was ushered into the office, a slightly different-looking Dyball from the one they had plucked from the toilet. Had his terror been genuine? His eyes were still wary, but now there was a sulky expression on his face. He hesitated only a moment before taking the seat before the desk.

'I don't have to tell you why you're here, Dyball.'

Beside Beamish's elbow was the recorder that was now compulsory in such interrogations. Before speaking he had switched it on, but it was doubtful if Dyball was aware of its significance. Then, with a glance at Gently, Beamish intoned the official caution.

'You understand, Dyball?'

Perhaps. The down-and-out merely stared.

'So. What have you got to say for yourself?'

For the moment, apparently nothing.

On the desk lay the contents of his pockets, which included three ten-pound notes. Beamish fingered them. 'Perhaps you'd like to tell us where this lot came from, Dyball?'

Dyball glanced at Gently, at the notes.

'Well?'

'There was this man . . .'

'Oh, pull the other one.'

'But there was! He said I could rent a room, that's why he gave me the money. A man . . .'

83

Beamish stared at the ceiling. 'And did he tell you his name was Rothschild?'

'He said . . .'

'Lay off it, Dyball. We know where these notes came from and so do you.'

'No!'

'Yes. It was time for you to hook it, so you grabbed these notes to help you on your way. Just before you had that marvellous sex change and went to crap in the ladies' toilet.'

'I never noticed . . .'

'Dyball!'

'But . . .'

'God give me patience.' Beamish sighed.

Gently said: 'There can be no question where the notes came from, Dyball. We found the money where you had hidden it, behind the cistern in the men's toilet.'

'But . . . I never knew nothing about that!'

'The fingerprints tell a different story.'

'No!'

'You hid the money there.'

'I didn't!'

'The money stolen from the coach was in your possession.'

Dyball stared at him wide-eyed, his mouth quivering. 'You – you're going to do me for this, aren't you?' he said. 'It don't matter what I say now, you're going to hang it all on me.'

Gently shrugged. 'Have you anything to say?'

'Yes . . . I never stole that money.'

'You didn't?'

'No – I found it. The bloke who took it must have thrown it away.'

'Thrown it . . . where?'

'In . . . in that rubbish bin, the one beside the shelter. I always poke around the bins, you can often find something there.'

'And you found the wallet. The package. The watch.'

84

'Yes, I'm telling you. Shoved in the bin . . .'

But Gently was shaking his head.

'I did!'

'No.'

'Well . . . that's all I'm going to say.'

Gently gazed at him. He said: 'Yesterday morning, at say around seven o'clock. Tell us where you were at that time, bearing in mind that we may have a witness.'

'A sodding . . . what?'

'Where were you, Dyball?'

'Me . . . I was dossing in the shelter.'

'No.'

'Yes, I never shifted till eight – it was then I found that gear in the rubbish-bin . . .'

'We have a witness, Dyball.'

'No, there was no one.'

'A witness who saw you leaving the coach. Pushing something into your pocket. And departing towards the town.'

'He never did.'

'Yes.'

'But . . .'

'A man who knows you by sight. Whose eye you caught as you were leaving. Whose signed statement is in our possession.'

'Oh gawd!'

'Do you wish to deny it?'

Now it wasn't only Dyball's mouth that was quivering. He sat staring helplessly at the desk, at the accusing notes lying on it.

'Have you anything to say?'

'Yes . . . it's his word . . .'

'Remember, you've been found in possession of the money.'

'You're going to do me, aren't you?'

Gently said nothing.

'But it wasn't me. It wasn't me!'

'Not . . . you?'

'I never killed him. It must have been the other bloke who did it and never found the money.'

'The other bloke . . .?'

'The one in the car. Only you're never going to believe me. I had the money and that's what counts. I should have known how it would finish up . . .'

'You are trying to tell me . . .?'

But, for the moment, Dyball could only snivel into unwashed hands.


'That money . . . I only took it to help give me a fresh start. Going to rent some lodgings, I was, so I could sign on and all that.'

Gently had ordered coffee and permitted Dyball to light a fag. For a space the recorder had been switched off, but now it was turning again. Dyball had drunk his coffee in a couple of gulps and was disposing of the fag in the same short order. 'In the summer it's all right, but later on . . .'

'If we can get back to yesterday, Mr Dyball.'

He stubbed out the fag. 'Got to tell you everything now, haven't I?'

'When you are ready.'

'Ah.' He looked wistfully at the cigarette packet. 'So I never slept in the shelter that night,' he said. 'It gets draughty down there sometimes and there's a better doss I know about. Are you on to me?'

Slowly, Gently nodded.

'There's the nets and old sacks,' Dyball said. 'You can make it cosy. And the blokes never say anything, not as long as you leave it tidy.'

'In fact, you slept in the net store.'

'I'm telling you, aren't I? They don't bother to lock the door.'

'The net store by the old coach?'

'Ah. They always lock that one down by the harbour.'

'Carry on.'

Dyball tugged at his beard. 'Can't tell you what time it

was,' he said. 'It was light, maybe after six, but I don't have a watch. Something woke me, this car pulling up across the road. I didn't pay much regard at first, just snugged down and kept comfortable, but then it struck me it might be the bloke who keeps his boat there, on an early start. So I get up and take a peek. And that's when I saw this other bloke. He came nipping out of the old coach, jumped in his car and drove off sharp. It struck me as rum. He'd left the door of the coach open and never stopped to belt up when he got in the car. He just reversed it hard and took off, towards Holmeness.'

Dyball paused, kept his eyes on the fag packet.

'Can you describe this man?' Gently said.

'Don't know that I can. Only it wasn't a fisherman. More like some of them you see around the town.'

'His age?'

Dyball shook his head. 'I never got a real look at him.'

'A tall man?'

'Taller than me. About your height, maybe.'

'Would you notice his clothes?'

'Like he wasn't a fisherman, I can't tell you much more than that.'

'Nothing that stood out.'

'A bit smartish, he looked, but nothing special that I can remember.'

Gently nodded. 'And the car?'

'That was one of them new Fiestas.'

'You – can be certain of that?'

'Ah, I can. I used to have one myself in the old days. I can't tell you the number of course, but that's what it was, one of them.'

'And . . . the colour?'

'Blue. Brand new it looked. I dare say it's one with the latest date letter.'

Gently paused, regarding Dyball. Then he said: 'Very well. Let us continue.'

Dyball met his eye, very briefly, then reapplied himself to his beard.

'I'd got a can and some grub . . . I went back inside and had my breakfast.'

'And then?'

'Well . . . it's like this. When I came back out, I could see that the door was still hung open.'

'The door of the coach?'

'Yes. It got me thinking. It could be the young fellow had cleared out . . .'

'So?'

'Well, I went to look, didn't I? By rights that coach belonged to me . . . So that's what I did. I went across there and peered round the door.'

'And Thorpe was dead.'

'Yes, he bloody was.'

'You are quite certain of that, Dyball?'

Dyball heaved on his beard.

'Perhaps you'll describe what you found there.'

'He – '

'Yes?'

'His bloody head was bashed in. That sod must have done it with the poker while the young fellow was asleep . . . He was on the bed with the sacks pulled over him; he couldn't have put up a fight. The bastard just went in there and did for him. He never gave the poor bugger a chance.'

'And you – what did you do?'

'Me? What could I do?'

'You could have contacted us and reported what you are telling us now. So why didn't you, Dyball?'

'Because – because – '

'Would it be because you didn't think we would believe you?'

'You know it sodding was.'

'And – perhaps – another reason?'

The beard was suffering.

'I told you. That money was no more use to him.'

'While, to you?'

'It meant everything. It was going to get me off the streets.'

'So – with the body still warm – you searched the coach to find the money.'

Dyball was snivelling. 'I didn't have to search – I'll never know why the other sod didn't take it. You could see his wallet sticking out under the pillow and you only had to feel a bit further . . . And his watch was on the stool, there was no reason to leave that . . .'

'Yet . . . the other man didn't take them?'

'It's bloody true! He may have been too scared . . .'

'But you weren't.'

'It wasn't me who killed him.'

'You were just the thief.'

'A bloke like me . . .'

Yes, a bloke like him. Gently gazed at the shrinking down-and-out. Beamish too. While the recorder turned. And Dyball wiped his nose with the sleeve of his coat.

'Listen, Dyball. Is there any good reason why we should accept this tale of yours?'

'I tell you it's true!'

'Listen. You knew that Thorpe was in possession of money, money that could get you off the streets and back to a respectable way of living. You knew where to find Thorpe, where you could have secure opportunity and, by your own account, you were present there at the time the crime was committed. We have a witness who can confirm that, and we find you in possession of Thorpe's money and effects. And we have no testimony of any other person in the neighbourhood at the time. Am I making it plain?'

'But that sod was there!'

'We have only your word for it.'

'He was. He bloody was.'

Gently shook his head. 'The certain facts are that you alone had knowledge, motive and opportunity. That being the case, it might be sensible if you acknowledged them and changed your story.'

89

'You mean – ?' His eyes were large.

'I think you know what I mean.'

'But – bloody hell!'

'Yes?'

The eyes stared, the mouth gaped among its beard. 'No. You go to hell!'

Gently shrugged. 'It might be best.'

'Yes – the best for you.'

'For you too.'

'For me, when I keep telling you?' His slumped figure jerked straight again. 'I never killed that bloke,' he said. 'Never. Never. I didn't. And that's all I'm going to say.'

'And your testimony of another man?'

'Just go to hell!'

'Did you or did you not see him?'

'You can think what you like.'

'The truth, Dyball.'

But Dyball's mouth shut like a trap.

'Then', Gently said, 'that's all for the present, Dyball.'

Dyball stared. 'I can bugger off?'

Gently shook his head. Beamish touched Dyball's shoulder.

'I think you may take your cigarettes,' Gently said.


He lit a pipe and strolled to the window, waiting for Beamish to return. On the pavements pedestrians, in formal dress, were already drifting towards the venue of the concert. Crime or not, the Festival proceeded and somewhere Capel was resining his bow ... one of the pedestrians was Madge Simpson, but she was alone. No sign of her distressed friend.

And ... Norton? By now, he should be in Bognor, inviting the condolence of his indignant wife ...

'What do you reckon, sir? Are we safe to do him?'

Were they? Gently shaped a ring. 'Perhaps we'll let him stew for a while. He knows now the size of the jam he is in.'

'You spelled it out for him, sir. And he wasn't too clever with that tale of his. If he really had seen another bloke, you'd think he could come up with a better description.'

'At the time, he may not have taken much notice.'

'You'd still think he could tell us a bit more. But no, he's just some cove who nips into his car and clears off.'

Gently puffed. 'He identified the car.'

'The first that came into his head, sir. And we know why. He used to own one. And probably that was a blue colour too.'

'It is a common car.'

'Too common, sir.'

'But – just suppose – he told the truth about that.'

'Sir?'

'We do know of someone who drives such a car, enamelled blue.'

Beamish stared. 'You can't mean . . .'

Gently nodded. 'Our friend Mr Norton. As you may remember, he arrived here this morning in a current model Fiesta.'

'Well, yes – he did, sir.'

'Perhaps a coincidence.'

'I dare say that's all it is, sir. Them being so common.'

'At the same time' – Gently puffed – 'if Dyball was telling us the truth, it might well fit. Robbery as a motive has always been questionable and Norton was unlikely to have taken the money.'

Beamish considered it, but shook his head. 'I still think Dyball was having us on, sir. It's the sort of tale you'd expect him to come up with – he got there second and only stole the dosh.'

'What description he gave would fit Norton?'

'Just that he was your height, sir.'

'We could still give the Sea View a call. To see what they remember about Norton that morning.'

But information from that quarter was equivocal. Certainly, Norton had requested an early breakfast and the waitress recalled him coming in from the terrace, but what time he rose and when he went out nobody was able to say. Nor would they have noticed a car being started, the parking being remote from the hotel – and furthermore, early deliveries were being made by vehicles that would have confused the issue.

'It doesn't tell us a lot, sir. Though it could have been him.'

'It is enough. We shall have to summon him back here.'

'I'll try his missus, sir. If that's where he went he should be there by now.'

Only he wasn't. And Mrs Norton was clearly becoming anxious. 'I was going to ring you myself . . . this isn't like Christopher at all. At any other time he would have been in touch. Are you quite certain you don't know where he is?'

'Could he have gone home, ma'am?'

'No. I've tried the flat and also the office. This just isn't like him. What have you done to him to make him behave in such a way?'

'I'm sorry, ma'am. But if he turns up . . .'

'Oh, don't worry. I know my duty.'

Beamish hung up, frowning, and repeated the conversation. 'It does begin to look a bit queer, sir.'

Yes. As though Norton had indeed taken off. In which case a general call would need to be put out. 'We'll give him a little longer. He may have had problems on the road.'

'You'd have thought he would have rung his missus.'

'He may be stuck where there isn't a phone.'

But Beamish was still frowning. Was it possible, after all, that it wasn't their man who was sitting in the cell . . . that a case, which had seemed so fire-proof, was about to take another turn?

'I should have put a man on him, sir. We had some goods on him before. And then, when he cleared off like that . . . We should have guessed from the way he was carrying on.'

Gently sighed. He was equally to blame.

92

'Perhaps another word with Dyball, sir?'

The down-and-out was fetched. His expression was sulky. His first act, on sitting down, was to light a cigarette, the next to blow smoke at them across the desk.

Beamish fixed him with a stern eye. 'Now, my man. We want the truth out of you. This bloke you pretend you saw. We want to hear a little more about him.'

Dyball exhaled smoke.

'You hear me, Dyball?'

'I aren't deaf, am I?' Dyball said.

'So what did he look like?'

'He'd got two legs.'

'Dyball!'

Dyball blew smoke.

'Dyball, you aren't helping yourself,' Beamish said. 'If you want us to believe in this bloke, you'd better answer the question. Was he fair? Was he dark? Did he have a moustache?'

'Two arms and two legs,' Dyball said. 'I saw him run to the car, didn't I? And then he drove of, so he had hands too.'

'Listen,' Gently said. 'We'd like to believe you, but you must help us with a little detail. That isn't too much to ask, is it? Try to visualise the man you saw there.'

'But I'm only pretending, aren't I?'

'Are you, Dyball?'

'Course I am. That's what he said.'

'There was no man? No car?'

Dyball blew smoke at Beamish. 'A bloke about your size,' he said. 'Up there on the road getting into his car. I could see he wasn't a fisherman and that's all I wanted to know.'

'A bit smartish, I think you said.'

'Well, he wasn't dressed like me.'

'But you remember his clothes?'

'I never noticed. Wearing a suit he was, maybe.'

'Not a zip-up jacket?'

Dyball looked vague. 'I tell you, he was way up there on the road. I only just got this peek at him, then he was in his car and away. Could have been what you say.'

'And the car – a Fiesta?'

'Right.'

'Parked facing towards the town?'

'Turned her, he did, backed her in, then headed off towards Holmeness. I could see he was in a hurry and I knew why when I looked in the coach.'

Gently nodded. 'Think carefully, Dyball. Is there anything else you can remember about him? Anything a little familiar, perhaps? As though you might have seen him before.'

'Like – someone I knew?'

Gently said nothing.

'Can't bring anyone to mind,' Dyball said. 'Could be I've seen him around, but there's plenty like him just now.'

Which was all they were going to get from Dyball.

'If only we can believe him, sir,' Beamish said, after he had ushered Dyball out. 'That guy would have to be Norton. It's just that Dyball is such a lousy bloody witness.'

'One problem. How the car was parked.'

'You mean – ?'

'It appears that it came from and returned to Holmeness.'

Beamish thought about it. 'Needn't be a problem, sir, it could just have been Norton acting crafty.'

Gently shrugged. Yes, it could. The drive round by Thwaite presented little obstacle. And that way he could have approached and departed from the scene with little risk of coming under observation.

'So – what we need now is to pull in Norton.'

The phone rang as he spoke.

'Police.'

'Listen, you sods! I'll ask you to just stop harassing my wife . . .'

'Norton?'

'Who else?'

'And where are you speaking from?'

'From here. From the Black Horse in Thwaite. Where I had to go for a room after you had me slung out of the Sea View. And if you bother my wife again . . .'

'Don't hang up, Mr Norton.'

## 7

'The concert starts in half an hour, so you'll bloody well have to wait till tomorrow.'

But Beamish had already ducked out of the office to dispatch a car to convey the estate agent.

'I am afraid we must insist, Mr Norton.'

'But what the hell do you want with me now? All right, I pissed off without telling you, but I'd have given you a ring – when I felt like it.'

'It would have helped if you had told us where you were going.'

'So I'm a bad boy. But must I miss the concert?'

'Regrettably, yes.'

'But for shit's sake can't it wait?'

'Unless you report to the police station we shall have no other option but to arrest you.'

'But . . . bloody why?'

'In the light of developments we require your assistance.'

'Developments – what lousy developments?'

'They will be explained when you arrive here.'

A pause. 'Is it something I may have seen?'

'When you get here, Mr Norton.'

Then the phone was slammed down at the other end.

A guilty man . . .? Gently frowned at the phone. More anger than fear had been the keynote of the exchange. To be missing a slice of the Wagner series had seemed to be what was uppermost in Norton's mind, an exasperation that he should be summoned for what seemed to him a trivial requirement . . .

'The patrol car will be there in minutes, sir. We had one stationed at The Maltings. I told them he was to drive his own car, with one of them holding his hand.'

'We will need an ID parade laid on.'

'Bidwell is on the job now.'

'And arrange for Dyball to get a look at the car – but not until Norton is safe in the office.'

'I'll have it put round the back, sir.'

'This one we play by the book.'

It was barely half an hour later when the blue Fiesta pulled in outside, with a patrol car on its heels, to be marshalled into the yard by a waiting uniformed man. Norton was brought in. Today he wore a tie, but was otherwise informally dressed. From his expression when he entered the office little of his anger had abated.

'Sit, Norton.'

'This had better be worth it. They'll have just started in back there.'

'You do realise that this is a serious matter?'

'So is Wagner – at least to some of us.'

He slammed himself down in the chair so lately vacated by Dyball, crossed his legs fiercely and stared from one to the other of them. 'If we could get this over before the interval . . .'

Gently nodded. 'We won't waste time. What we have to ask you refers to the events of yesterday morning.'

'But sod it, we've been through all that! You've got my statement there in front of you.'

'A statement that describes your walk to Thwaite.'

'Signed, sealed and delivered. So what the hell do you want now?'

'A little more.'

'But what?'

'About your movements prior to that walk.'

Norton stared. 'You're off your loaf. All I did before that was have my breakfast.'

'All, Norton?'

'Yes – all. Apart from having my bath and getting dressed.'

'And if you were seen re-entering the hotel?'

'I was never out of it. Except for a breather while they fried my bacon.'

The recorder was turning.

'But – earlier still?'

Norton glared at him. 'Just what are you getting at?'

'I'm getting at this,' Gently said. 'We have received certain information. About a person answering your description driving a car identical to your own, seen prior to the time when you had your breakfast. What do you have to say to that?'

'Say? What should I bloody say?'

'Were you out in your car at that time, Norton?'

'Was I, hell! The answer is no.'

'The description fits you.'

Norton spat. 'Well?' His glare was ferocious. 'And this is the sodding reason, is it – the reason why I'm missing my concert? What bastard was it who told you this?'

'A witness we can place.'

'Place – where?'

'At a critical place. At a critical time.'

'But bloody where?'

'Are you sure you don't know?'

Suddenly his eyes were widening. 'You can't mean . . .?'

Gently nodded.

'Oh, my God!'

'Do you understand now?'

'Understand! That some lying sod . . .'

'But would he really have been lying, Norton?'

'Lying – yes? Lying his head off. And are we certain it was a him and not a her?'

Gently shrugged. 'Forget Miss Ford. And our witness has no connection with the lady. He was a person demonstrably present at that time, in a situation from which he could observe the event.'

'And he's saying I was there?'

'This is what he is saying. That he heard a car pull in at the coach and that, supposing it to be someone known to him, he went to look in that direction. It was not that person. The man he describes bears a credible resemblance

99

to yourself and the car he was driving was a blue Fiesta of the current model, like your own.'

'You're kidding me – this can't be true.' In his eyes, both fear and indignation. 'You're trying it on.'

'No.'

'Yes. Ask at the hotel. They'll tell you . . .'

Gently shook his head. 'We have enquired there. They could tell us only that you were seen re-entering the hotel and that your car was parked at a distance from it, while other vehicles were in use at that time.'

'But they must have bloody known!'

Gently said nothing.

Fear was now the dominant factor in the staring grey eyes. 'So – what else did this sod see?'

'When he saw him, the man was at that moment coming out of the coach. He appeared in a great hurry and left the door ajar behind him. Then he jumped into his car and drove off with equal haste.'

'And it was me – I'd just killed Thorpe?'

'Is that a question, or an admission?'

'Sod you, I never drove my car yesterday – I hiked to Thwaite and got a lift back. Can you prove different?'

Gently watched him.

'Hear me tell you,' Norton snarled. 'If it's true what this swine is saying, then it wasn't me and it wasn't my car. It was someone else, get me? Fiestas are a dime a dozen and blue is the favourite colour. And that's all you've got that connects me with him.'

'You deny being that man?'

'Yes. Yes, I do. And I'd like to get back to my concert at Thwaite . . .'

Gently sighed and shook his head.

'You mean you are going to hold me here?'

'I mean there is a certain preliminary, which I must ask you to undertake.'

'What sodding preliminary?'

'One that is essential. You must attend an identity parade.'

100

'But bloody hell!'

'You object to that?'

Indignation had overcome fear. 'So play your stupid little games if you must – and see what that's going to buy you.'

'You consent to the parade?'

'Do I have an option?'

'I regret not.'

Norton spat.


'Dyball picked out the car directly, sir, only that doesn't mean very much.'

In reception the prospects were being assembled for the parade that was to follow: men in their thirties or thereabouts, few of whom bore any great resemblance to Norton. Only two approached him in height and build, and both, from their dress, suggested manual workers.

'It was the best we could do at short notice, sir. There's a couple more to come. In the normal way we could put in some of our chaps, but you'd never fool Dyball with them.'

Meanwhile Norton was detained in the office, with DC Stubbs to keep him company. He had shifted his chair across to the window and sat staring at the world without. A world shortly to be exchanged for a prison cell...? Gently was unable to make up his mind. There was something about Norton... The facts were mounting against him, yet still Gently didn't feel comfortable. His manner, that vein of indignation ... fear, but not guilt. Wasn't that where it lay?

'We're about ready, sir. Shall we have him in?'

The prospects were lined up in reception. Norton was fetched and given his instructions. He chose a place as near as possible to the centre of the line-up. Then Dyball, who had been briefed previously, but still seemed uncertain about the part he had to play.

'Who are these buggers ...?'

'Never you mind! Just go over there and do what we told you.'

'But there's some who know me . . .'

'Do it, Dyball!'

'Well, if you say . . .'

Unhappily, he shambled over to the line-up and began to make his way along it, nervously glancing at the faces presented to him, one or two of which were grinning. A pause at Norton? If so, the glare he received quickly moved him on. But, on the return trip, at the rear of the line, the pause was more prolonged. Was he going to touch him? His hand was raised, then he stared up at Norton's head and the hand dropped again. Why? He was frowning to himself as he completed his tour of the line. With a final glance at Norton, he shambled back to his watchful mentors.

'Well?'

'That bloke over there . . .'

'Are you telling us he was the one?'

'It could have been . . . but his hair . . .'

'His hair?'

'The bloke I saw was bald.'

'Bald!' Beamish glared. 'And now you remember it?'

'I see his head when he ducked into the car.'

'Dyball, if you're lying – '

'A bit older he was, too.'

And from that they couldn't shift him: he recalled the low dawn sun glinting on the man's pate; a hundred, a hundred and fifty yards distant, but for a moment the gleam had caught his eye . . . a gleam that couldn't have originated with Norton, whose bush of curly dark hair was such a prominent feature. The truth? Or was Norton a man who might be good for a future touch . . . ? There were two other possibilities in the line-up, but only Norton had caught Dyball's eye.

102

'What do you reckon, sir?'

Gently shook his head. Without testimony from Dyball, Norton was in the clear – fear, but not guilt. While suspect two, Dyball, had apparently ignored a golden chance to take the heat off himself . . . A terrible liar was what Capel had called him. If so, he had carried it off with considerable aplomb.

'Let's have Norton back in.'

There was a glint in the estate agent's eye as he entered.

'So it didn't work, did it.'

'Please take a seat, Norton.'

'Here, you'd better pull my hair – just to make sure it isn't a wig.'

He sat, this time sprawling, and tilted his chin at Gently across the desk. Clearly he felt he had been exonerated by the down-and-out's failure to identify him.

Gently gave him a stare and said: 'The matter isn't quite finished with yet, Norton. The witness isn't noted for his veracity and it was you he singled out.'

'And then he changed his mind.'

'He could change it again.'

'Come off it, you know he couldn't make it stick.'

'Also, he identified your car correctly.'

'Yes – the commonest car on the road.'

'Including the correct model and colour.'

'Watch the next one that passes in the street.'

'Yet . . . why should he choose that one, out of all the others he might have picked on? And a man who differs from you only in having lost some hair?'

'Leave it out,' Norton said. 'Leave it out. He was telling a tale and you know it. If he was anywhere near that coach at the time he would have to come up with something. So he did and it put you on to me. But I was still in bed when all that was happening.'

'Which you can't prove.'

'And which I don't have to.'

Gently stared at him. And Norton stared back.

But then, suddenly, something seemed to strike Norton and his stare became a frown. He looked away, at the window, but finally shook his head.

'Well?'

'Just an idea. There probably isn't anything in it.'

'Still?'

'You would only tell me I was trying to shift the blame.'

'Nevertheless, I would like to hear it.'

Norton scowled at nothing. 'All right, then. It's about Yvonne.'

'About your sister . . .?'

'Yes, Yvonne. We used to do everything together, even after she was married. When I swopped my car last August, Yvonne swopped hers too – same make, same model, same colour. Back there at the Windmill there's a car like mine.'

'A car like yours . . .'

Norton bit his lip.

'And you are suggesting?'

'I'm suggesting nothing. Just that there are other cars like mine. And you can make what you like of that.'

Gently went on watching him.

Norton no longer sprawled. He sat with his hands clasped between his knees. His eyes were narrowed, fixed on the desk, his mouth set in a tight line. 'That secretary of his . . .'

Gently was silent.

'It was she who spotted Thorpe, wasn't it? And you can bet who she'd get in touch with – probably before she reported it to you. Isn't that likely?'

Gently shrugged.

'Yes, twice likely,' Norton said. 'She treats him like a god. She could have warned Yvonne never to marry him, but did she? Not on your life.'

'I'm afraid this proves nothing . . .'

'But it's a fact. Oswald knew where he could find Thorpe. And if a car like mine was really seen at the coach, then Oswald had a car like mine he could have used.' His eyes

104

met Gently's. 'Have you seen his own car? It's a Mondeo that stands out a mile...'

Gently shook his head.

Norton stared at the desk again. 'Perhaps he didn't mean to kill him,' he said. 'Perhaps he just meant to rough him up before he handed him over to you lot. But then again, if he used Yvonne's car... And I know, if you don't, that it wasn't mine...'

'Could have a point, sir,' Beamish said. 'Only Hastings was in London and yours truly was here.'

Norton dealt him a dirty look.

'And chummie, he was AWOL, while Hastings was still tucked up in bed.'

Norton spat. 'I might have known. I'm just wasting my time talking to you. So think what you like. But bear in mind you can't prove a bloody thing.'

'Perhaps not yet,' Beamish said. 'Not yet.'

Norton scowled at him and spat again. 'So it's still got to be me,' he said. 'I'm still Number One on your list. I opened my mouth too wide back in town and now you aren't going to look any further.' He thrust his chin out at Gently. 'Are you locking me up?'

Gently shrugged. 'Is that an admission?'

'No it sodding isn't.'

'In that case, Mr Norton...' Gently regarded him sternly for a moment. He said: 'I think you understand that your situation is one that we can't entirely ignore and that for the present we cannot allow you to absent yourself from these parts.'

'In other words...'

'You will be under surveillance. We shall return you to your lodging at Thwaite, but your car will remain here and observation will be kept on your movements. And we require your solemn word that you will hold yourself at our disposal. Understood?'

Norton's mouth was grim. 'Do I have any frigging option?'

Gently shook his head.

After a pause, Norton spat once more and jerked himself to his feet.

'So where does that leave us, sir?'

Gently was wondering the same thing. While Beamish was arranging the dispatch of Norton he had lit a pipe and sat gloomily smoking it. On the one hand the lying Dyball, found in possession of the cash; on the other the irascible estate agent, devoid of any acceptable alibi . . .

And the ID parade, had it told them anything other than that Dyball and the truth had never been bedfellows?

'I was a bit surprised you let him go, sir. Ten to one Dyball's going to change his mind. He picked the right bloke, then he had second thoughts, but a night in the cells should improve his memory. What do you think?'

Gently breathed smoke.

'I like Norton,' Beamish said. 'The car and all. Everything's going for him. Like the state Thorpe was in when we found him. You wouldn't expect that sort of thing from Dyball.'

Gently shrugged. 'But Dyball had the money.'

'It could have been the way he said. If he did go in there after Norton left, you wouldn't expect him to leave it behind.'

'The trouble with Dyball is believing him.'

'Now and then he lets the truth slip, sir.'

'But when?'

Beamish shook his head. 'I can see your point, sir. But I still fancy Norton, when all's said and done. Like just now when you were putting him through it and he tried to shove Mr Hastings at us. He's worried, sir, we're getting too close to him. And if Dyball should change his mind . . .'

Gently puffed. 'Dyball offered a description.'

'One he made up off the cuff, sir. Like he could see it might be worth his while to give Norton a hand-up.'

106

'Did nothing else occur to you?'

'Sir?'

'Mr Hastings was in here this morning.'

'Mr Hastings . . .?'

Gently nodded. 'It may have escaped your attention, but he is about the same build as his brother-in-law and has begun to go bald on top.'

Beamish stared. 'You aren't serious, sir.'

Gently shrugged. 'Perhaps a coincidence. But it certainly seemed to be Norton's hair that was making up Dyball's mind for him.'

'It's what gave him the idea, sir.'

'You could be right. Or perhaps the hair, for once, surprised the truth from him.'

'Just gave him the notion, sir, that's all. You can't really believe Mr Hastings had a hand in it.'

Gently nostrilled smoke. Could he believe it? As against the situation of the other two prospects . . . That the prosperous tycoon, on a doubtful word from his secretary, would drive down from Wimbledon to seek his revenge? No, if the man had really been Thorpe, then his arrest would have satisfied Hastings . . .

The similarity of cars had given Norton an opening, but that was all one could read into that.

Gently glanced at his watch. 'He is probably at home – and I promised to ring him if we found the money.'

'You aren't going to mention, sir . . .?'

Gently shook his head. 'Hand me the file – it should have his number.'

He dialled and the phone was answered promptly.

'Hastings here . . .'

'Chief Superintendent Gently.'

'Oh . . .' There was a moment's pause. 'Then you have some news for me?'

'The news I promised. We have found the missing money.'

'The money.'

107

'It is mostly intact, give or take a couple of hundred. At the moment it's required as evidence, but we should be able to release it shortly.'

Another pause. 'And – the thief?'

'The man found in possession is under lock and key. More than that for the moment I can't tell you, except that we are following up the testimony he gave us.'

'The testimony? But surely he's your man.'

'As I said, for the moment I may not tell you.'

'But for heaven's sake – if you found him with the money?'

'I can only repeat that we are pursuing his testimony.'

A further pause.

'Look,' Hastings said. 'I don't expect you to give away confidential information, but I do have a personal interest in this and you could be a little more forthcoming. If the man who had the money isn't the culprit, has he given you a lead to who might be?'

Now it was Gently's turn to pause. 'Perhaps I may go as far as this. Our investigation points in more than one direction and certain leads we have are being actively dealt with.'

'Certain leads . . .'

'I cannot be specific.'

'Am I allowed to make a guess?'

'I think, perhaps – '

'No, listen. You know very well whom I have in mind. And if you haven't charged the man you found with the money, then the odds are he is pointing you at someone else. Am I far out?'

Gently was silent.

'Good enough,' Hastings said. 'Ever since I heard he was present in Shinglebourne I felt convinced that he was your man. And my guess is you've got him under wraps, but don't worry, I won't push you any further.'

Gently said: 'I am mentioning no names.'

'With me, you don't have to.'

'Simply, that we have certain leads.'

108

'Leads, yes.' Did he hesitate?

'In the meantime, Mr Hastings, I can promise you early information of our progress and I must ask you to keep to yourself any suppositions that may occur to you.'

'Yes . . . understood.'

'I suppose I may reach you at your office?'

'My office . . . yes, most days. Though occasionally I'm out visiting clients. Yesterday I was in Milton Keynes, discussing a campaign with Magnum Breweries.'

'With . . . Magnum Breweries.'

'Perhaps you know them. But most days you'll find me in the office.'

'Thank you, Mr Hastings.'

'And about the money – well, no hurry.'

Gently hung up. Yesterday . . . And had he needed to give chapter and verse?

'Any luck, sir?' Beamish asked. 'You were pushing him a bit, with those leads.'

Gently shrugged and relit his pipe. 'Just a couple of loose ends,' he said.

'Loose ends, sir?'

'The smell of an alibi, but we'd better check it out. Tomorrow we'll get in touch with a brewery in Milton Keynes and have a man visit Hastings's office.'

'An alibi, sir.'

'I said the smell of one. It could offer cover for a trip out this way. But that's all. For the rest, we're back with trying to believe Dyball.'

'We could have him back in, sir . . .'

Gently sighed and shook his head. 'We'll leave him to ponder in his cell.'

A long day.

And not quite over yet . . .

As Gently was leaving, the telephone rang.

'It's the secretary, sir.'

Gently took it. At the other end, heavy breathing and sobs.

'Miss Ford?'

'It was him again. He's just been on the phone . . .'

'Are we talking of Norton?'

'Yes – him. And he's saying . . . oh, I can't repeat it.'

'He is saying what, Miss Ford?'

'About the car – it was seen there. And Oswald! Oh, I can't go on. He says now you think . . . that you believe . . .'

'He spoke of Mr Hastings?'

'And he blames me for everything, because I told Oswald whom I'd seen. And then Oswald – oh, it's impossible. You can't believe that – tell me you can't.'

'Please calm down, Miss Ford . . .'

'Tell me!'

'You are upsetting yourself without cause.'

'But he said you had a witness – someone who'd seen him.'

'We have no immediate reason to think – '

'It wasn't him – it couldn't have been him. Tell me – please tell me.'

'I repeat, we have no immediate reason to believe that your employer was involved in the case.'

She calmed down in the end, though the sobs were never far away. It wasn't true then – it was only the car and Norton believing what he wanted to believe. He wanted to upset her, but it wasn't true. He hated her because she should have warned his sister . . .

'If he rings you again, refer him to me.'

'But suppose he comes round here . . .'

'That won't happen.'

'I'm sorry, but he hates me so much.'

'Just leave the matter with us, Miss Ford.'

Gently hung up and wiped his brow.

Beamish was grinning. 'Quite a card, that secretary.'

'Give Norton a ring – right now.'

'Right you are, sir.' Beamish made a face. 'And my money is still on that one, sir.'

# 8

A long day – and a troubled night, tossing and turning in the bedroom at Heatherings. Always the picture at Shingle-bourne was changing, shifting emphasis, direction. The first bold strokes had been laid in Putney in that pleasant basement flat by the Thames, simple, straightforward, explicable, the deed and the culprit not in question. But then action had shifted to the Festival town and at once the questions began to mount: a deed of robbery? Of revenge? Or was there some other element yet unidentified?

The beggar, the brother, the shadow of the husband ... to which of these was the finger pointing? And, in the wings, the hysterical secretary ... but could a full stop be placed there?

Dyball alone held the foreground, by testimony and admission placed at the scene, and with the loot in his possession; but also with a tale not entirely incredible. Next the brother, glanced at by Dyball; and finally the husband, implicated by both of them. If it ended there, which? And if it didn't, then ... then ...?

Behind all that, was there still something else: a factor he sensed but which was eluding him?

He couldn't decide. All night, it seemed, the matter was turning over in his brain, beginning with the scene at the flat in Putney, but, in the end, getting him nowhere. If such an angle existed then he was missing it. Anxiety alone had been the enemy of his slumber ...

'Did you have a rough night, Mr George?'

Grumpily he received his cup of tea from Mrs Jarvis. She drew the bedroom curtains for him and the early sun made him wince.

'I heard you tossing about in here ...'

He felt for his pipe, which he rarely lit before breakfast.

111

Something must have occurred to him – what was it? But if so, he had forgotten it now.

'Shall I expect you tonight, Mr George?'

'I'll give you a ring . . .'

'You won't mind if it's only an omelette?'

Really he couldn't have cared less.

Something . . .

He took his shower and almost forgot to shave; ate his breakfast in glum silence and ignored the papers that Mrs Jarvis brought him. Unlocking his car, he paused. Could it have been that, to do with the cars . . .? But finally he shook his head, belted up and got on the road.


'I've had another go at Dyball, sir, and now he isn't so sure about that bloke. Says the sun shining on his hair may have given him the idea he was bald.'

Gently shrugged. 'At your suggestion?'

'Well . . . I may have given him a hint, sir.'

'But he still doesn't go overboard on Norton?'

'No, not yet, sir. But we're making progress.'

Gently shrugged again. Progress of a sort. 'Did you have a word with Norton?'

'Yes, sir, I told him off proper for him having a go at Miss Ford. He's really into that girl; he swears she knows more than she's telling us, like she could help us nab Hastings. But that's only what you would expect.'

'And the latest report?'

'Nothing special, sir. He had his breakfast and strolled down to The Maltings and went to look at an exhibition of pictures. I warned our man to keep a close eye on him, in case he slinks out by a different exit.'

'Find the number of that brewery Hastings mentioned.'

After a while, he got through to the office. 'George Gently here. Am I right in thinking that Oswald Hastings is with you this morning?'

'Mr Hastings? No, I'm sorry. It was two mornings ago when he was here.'

'Two mornings ago?'

'Yes, I'm afraid so. We were surprised, too. We weren't expecting him till Friday, but he rang and asked if we minded bringing it forward.'

'He rang from his office?'

'No, I don't think so, it sounded like he was in a call-box. It could be that someone else had let him down and since he was in the district he called us.'

'This was in the morning?'

'Yes, quite early. If you'd rung then you would have got him.'

'Oswald in his Mondeo . . .'

'I see you know him. But no, he was driving something more modest, don't ask me what.'

'I expect the Fiesta. What colour was it?'

'Blue . . . I think. But that's all I can tell you.'

Gently sighed. 'Thanks, anyway. No doubt I'll catch up with him some time.'

'If you need his office number . . .'

'Thank you. I already have it.'

He hung up.

Beamish was watching him with a roguish glint in his eye. 'That was a cunning one, sir. And did it get us a line on him?'

'A bit of a line.'

He repeated what the girl in the office had told him.

Beamish was frowning. 'So, like that, we could have Hastings in the frame too . . .'

'It's still circumstantial.'

'But if he was driving that car, sir.'

'It may only have been because his own was in for a service.'

'And then, him ringing from a box . . .'

'The girl suggested a possible reason for that.'

'But you'd think he'd have a mobile.'

Gently shrugged. 'He may have left it in the other car.'

Beamish shook his head, unconvinced – two ways there might be, but adding it together? Clearly, for Beamish,

Norton had begun to drift a little in the reckoning. 'You can't deny he had motive, sir, it being his missus who was done for. And after his secretary rang him he knew where to lay hands on the bloke. So he switches cars, drives out here, finds the place as he thinks deserted – nothing to stop him. Then, after the job is done, he has to have a reason for not turning up at his office.'

Yes – that was the case. But was it one that fitted the man? Fitted a tough, prospering business tycoon who weighed every move before he acted on it? Revenge he may have wanted, but not the risk of a personal involvement. A life sentence for the culprit should have satisfied Hastings. And if it did not? For the moment one could only shake one's head.

'We shall have to check further. Though it may be tricky.'

'We could have that secretary back in, sir.'

'First, a delicate enquiry at the office in Fulham, to see what did happen there that morning.'

A job for his sidekick, Dutt, who could be relied on not to put his foot in it. On the phone Gently gave him careful instructions, emphasising the grounds for caution.

'No need to worry about that, sir. I made some pals the last time we were there.'

'Think up a tale to excuse your enquiries.'

'Leave it to me, sir, I won't let you down.'

Gently left it with him. He filled and lit his pipe.

Beamish fiddled with a ball-pen on the desk. 'Dyball, sir,' he said at last. 'Perhaps we should be keeping the heat on him.'

Slowly Gently nodded. Any case against Hastings rested on Dyball.

'I'll fetch him – '

'Wait.'

'Sir?'

Gently blew smoke. 'An outing may be more productive. A little trip to the net store on the beach could be of assistance to Dyball's memory.'

Beamish stared. 'If you say so, sir.'

'Just us and him. And Norton's car.'

'I'll fetch the key, sir.'

Five minutes later, the Fiesta was heading out towards Holmeness.


In the direction of the town there were one or two strollers, but otherwise they had the beach to themselves, warm under the August sun, the only sound the murmur of breakers. Beamish turned the car and parked it facing towards the town, at a guess one hundred and fifty yards from the little hut across the road.

'Out you get, my man.'

The purpose of the visit had been explained to Dyball. He climbed out of the car a little stiffly and stood staring at the coach and its fence of ribbons. 'He isn't still in there is he . . .?'

Beamish rolled his eyes at Gently.

'I mean, you aren't going to make me . . .'

'On your way, sonny-boy.'

He was escorted across the road, and down to the beach and the hut. The fishing boat was absent and the door of the hut, which faced the sea, was ajar. From there, a few tumps of marram-grass screened the actual road itself, but the car was plainly visible on its parking before the coach.

Curiously, Dyball peered into the hut. 'There aren't many nets . . .'

'Never mind them, Dyball.'

'But if you're dossing here – '

'Listen, sunshine, just where were you when you saw that man?'

Dyball fingered his beard. 'Like where you're standing. I just came out and stuck my head round . . . I mean, if it had been that fisher bloke . . .'

'Never mind him – you come and stand here.'

Dyball shuffled to the spot, a couple of yards from the door. From there, leaning a little to the right, the coach and the car were fully visible.

115

'Now, my lad, we'll take it from there. You tell us exactly what you saw.'

'The car, I see that, didn't I, and the bloke – '

'Hold on. What car?'

'W . . . that car. The one that's there now.'

'You're quite sure of that, Dyball?'

He looked puzzled. 'W'yes. Isn't that the car I saw?'

'I'm asking you, Dyball.'

He shook his head. 'Of course, I never did see the number. But that's the one, the latest model, same colour and all that.'

'And you recognised it – a Ford Fiesta?'

'Didn't I say so from the start?'

'You could tell that from here?'

'Ah, I told you. I always keep an eye on them things.'

Beamish eyed him narrowly. 'So carry on, sunshine. You saw that car parked up there. What happened next?'

'W'then the bloke came out, and got in the car and drove away.'

'The bloke like Norton.'

'Ah, him.'

'But who wasn't Norton.'

'Well . . . right up there . . .'

Gently said: 'Describe him again, this man you saw coming out of the coach.'

Dyball hesitated, his eyes staring. He shuffled his feet in the sand.

'Come out in a hurry, didn't he,' he said. 'He was down to the car before you could blink. A tallish sort of bloke, he was, and when he lumped in the car you could see it wobbling. I tell you what, he never belted up, just slammed the door and started her going – backed her in there, he did, and you could see the muck fly as he drove off.'

'A tallish sort of man.'

'About your size, I reckon, the way he stooped to get in the car.'

'Did you notice his clothes?'

'Blast no, but I could see he wasn't a fisherman.'

116

'More like a holiday-maker.'

'Could have been. I can't tell you more than that.'

'And his face?'

Dyball shook his head. 'He was too far off up there, wasn't he?'

'But – something else you did notice?'

Dyball shuffled a foot. 'When he was getting in the car,' he said. 'When he stooped. But I aren't going to swear to it, like it could have been the sun on his brilliantine.'

Gently said: 'When you came to Norton in the line-up it was his bushy hair that made you doubtful. Wouldn't that be because the man you saw had hair that was sparse and perhaps receding?'

Dyball felt his beard. 'Ah. Could be.'

'I think the answer is yes, Dyball.'

Dyball stared towards the car. 'But I can't swear to it – not with him up there and me down here. I just caught that one look, when he was stooping into his car, that's when I saw something. It could have been as you say.'

'A gleam that suggested baldness.'

Dyball tugged his beard.

'Very well,' Gently said. 'A little experiment. I will ask Inspector Beamish to play the part of the man you saw. He will go back to the coach and you will see him emerge from it, run to the car and throw himself into the driver's seat. The inspector is about the height of the man you describe and' – he shrugged apologetically – 'bears another resemblance. Do you understand?'

Dyball stared. 'But he isn't like him . . .'

'Near enough,' Gently said. 'And the sun may be higher, but it's still in a direction that should serve our purpose.'

He signalled to Beamish, who gave a grimace and set off back towards the coach. They saw him unlock it, push the door ajar and stand in the entry, looking back towards them. Gently raised his hand. Beamish bolted out, ran to the car and threw open the door. Then, as he bent to jump in, his head jerked back. And there was the gleam.

'Well?'

117

Dyball was gazing. 'But that sod . . . it could have been him.'

'That was what you saw?'

'Ah. It's only the clothes . . . the clothes were different . . .'

'The – clothes?'

He nodded. 'Darker they were . . . I'm trying to think. Like a suit he must have had on, something smart . . . the sort they wear in court . . .'

'A business suit?'

'What they wear . . . seeing him brought it back . . .'

'And the other?'

'Like I said. When he was getting into the car . . .'

'In so many words, that man wasn't Norton?'

Dyball shook his head. 'Couldn't have been him. This one was different . . . older . . .' His eyes squeezed tight. 'I can see him, now.'

'And that you will swear to?'

'I'll swear it.'

He gave a fierce tug to his tangled beard.


On that he didn't go back; in the office he signed an amended statement. The man was balding, wore a city suit and was visibly older than Christopher Norton.

'I suppose we have to believe him, sir?'

'I think this time he is telling the truth.'

A truth that pointed in only one direction, however improbable it might at first have seemed. From the shadowy margins of the case the figure of Oswald Hastings had begun to stand out. Hate must be supposed to have overcome caution, the desire for revenge his personal peril. When information had arrived he had played it down, but already the fever was stirring in his soul . . .

A credible picture?

Beamish was looking blank. 'I mean, when you start looking round it, sir. One can believe that sort of thing of Norton, but it's another matter with Hastings. And Norton,

118

he was here on the spot, while Hastings was up in London. And Dyball, he's such a liar, he could just be telling us what he thinks we want to hear.'

Gently shook his head. 'Not in my opinion. Our little game gave his memory a jolt. And Hastings was on the loose somewhere that morning. Though he may have an explanation for that.'

'So there you are, sir. We could never prove it and we'd be mad to produce Dyball in court. If Hastings really was the bloke we can pack the case in right here.'

'Not quite so soon.'

'We may as well, sir. Unless you reckon we have a chance with Norton.'

'Dyball's testimony rules him out.'

'Perhaps it was Dyball all the time, sir.'

Yes ... with Dyball there was at least a case: presence, motive and even evidence. While as a witness against a third party, any defence counsel would make hay of him. But ...

The telephone rang. 'Dutt here, sir. I ran your little errand.'

'And?'

'You were dead right, sir. Hastings never showed up there that morning.'

'Did he ring the office?'

'Yes, sir. And I talked to the girl who took the message. He said to tell them he wouldn't be in that day because he was visiting the client in Milton Keynes.'

'A call from a phone box?'

'No question about that, sir. He ran out of change and got cut off.'

'Did he show up at all that day?'

'Just before closing, she says.'

'Later, we may need a statement from her.'

'Shouldn't be any trouble about that, sir.'

Gently hung up.

Beamish said: 'Any luck, sir?'

119

Gently nodded. 'It fits in. Though it could still be perfectly innocent. Except the little matter of him using his wife's car.'

'It could be like you said, sir, and his own was in dock.'

Or it could have been merely a whim, a sentimental gesture. But was Hastings a man to have such whims, especially when visiting important clients? Somehow, Gently didn't think so. And the tycoon's relations with his wife had been less than cordial.

Perhaps time for a word with the secretary . . .? 'Send a man round to the White Hart.'

'Yes, sir, I was going to suggest it. If anyone can give us a line, it's her.'


Bidwell fetched her.

She arrived in the office with a certain sullenness in her mien, an air of determination, and took her seat without being requested. She looked firmly across at Gently. 'Am I brought here to be told that you've arrested him?'

'Arrested whom, Miss Ford?'

'The brother, of course. Can there be any doubt that he's the one you are after?'

'There has been no arrest.'

'But surely! He as much as admitted to me he was the culprit and was blaming me for giving him away. I felt certain by now you'd have him under arrest.'

'He – made an admission?'

'Well, near enough! That you made him stand in an identity parade, because someone like him had been seen leaving the coach, and that then you had set a detective to watch him to make quite certain he didn't run away. Isn't that what happened?'

'Routine measures were taken.'

'Yet still you haven't arrested him?'

'The matter is under review, Miss Ford. You may rely on us to take any appropriate action.'

'But he did it. I know he did it.'

'You know – ?'

'It has to be him. Nobody else would do a thing like that, it stands out a mile. So why are you waiting?'

Gently shrugged and shook his head.

'And it doesn't matter that he's threatening me?'

'That is being taken care of, Miss Ford.'

'But why – tell me why! – haven't you arrested him?'

She sat staring, clutching the bag on her lap, her painted lips beginning to quiver. And on her brow now was a misty gleam of perspiration. 'You must have a reason.'

Gently said: 'We have requested your presence for quite another purpose, Miss Ford. I would like to take you back to the occasion when you sighted Thorpe at the coach. You appeared uncertain whether to report it and asked advice of your friend. Then, still uncertain, you rang your employer and put the same question to him. At what time would that have been?'

A flicker in the eyes. 'Why are you asking me about this?'

'You do remember, Miss Ford?'

'Of course I do. But I can't see – '

'If you would just answer the question.'

'Oh, very well. It was in the evening, after dinner at the hotel. I rang him at home, in Wimbledon, on the off-chance I would find him in.'

'And you told him you had seen Thorpe?'

'I told him I'd seen someone who looked like him.'

'Who looked like him?'

'Yes, I couldn't be certain, I only had that glimpse of him as we drove past.'

'He was a person familiar to you, Miss Ford.'

'I can't help that, it was just a glimpse.'

'Yet you couldn't dismiss it from your mind.'

'How could I, the way things were? I wanted to. I could see it might land me in trouble if I reported it, but I felt I had to do something. That's the only reason I rang Mr Hastings.'

'He would be concerned to hear what you told him.'

121

'Naturally. What else could you expect?'

'He questioned you closely.'

'I suppose so. But I couldn't tell him any more than I've told you.'

'So . . . he remained unconvinced.'

'Yes. Yes, he did.'

'He advised you not to act too hastily.'

'To sleep on it, that's what he told me, and to see how I felt about it the next day.' She wrestled with the handbag, her mouth tremulous. 'But why are you asking me all this again? I told you before and gave it to you in my statement. There really is nothing else for me to tell you.'

Gently watched her a moment, then nodded. 'As you know, Miss Ford, your employer paid us a visit here yesterday. The car he was driving was a bright-red Mondeo. Can you confirm it is the car he usually makes use of?'

Her eyes flickered again – widened. 'The car – ?'

'Yes. Your employer's car, Miss Ford.'

'No. No – he doesn't always use that one. He has a smaller one he drives.'

'A smaller car?'

'Yes – a Fiesta.'

'The same colour as the other?'

'No – blue. Blue.'

'It could not be mistaken for the Mondeo?'

She shook her head wildly, staring past him.

'One other thing,' Gently said. 'In the conversation on the phone with your employer. Did you happen to describe in detail the spot where you thought you had caught sight of Thorpe?'

'No, never. I didn't.'

'No mention of the coach?'

'No.'

'He didn't ask for particulars?'

'No . . . no!'

'And you gave him none?'

She burst into tears. 'You can't be thinking this – you can't! You've just brought me here to try it on. It must be

122

something the brother has been telling you – he's wicked, wicked. And you know he did it.'

'And you deny giving details to Mr Hastings.'

'Yes, a thousand times.' She sobbed. 'The idea that Oswald – oh, it's preposterous, you can't be serious. You can't . . .'

'In your opinion he wouldn't do such a thing?'

'Oswald? No. No!'

'He would have no motive for such a deed?'

'You can't think that just because – '

'Because what, Miss Ford?'

'Because!'

She dashed tears from her eyes.

'Well?'

'Oh, I've said too much already. You'll just have to think what you like.'

'That . . . such a motive may perhaps have existed?'

'Think what you like. But none of it's true.'

'You are unwilling to assist us.'

'I've said all I'm going to say.'

The tears flooded back uncontrollably and her handbag slipped from her knees to the floor.


'She's a liar, sir. And she fancies him.'

The sobbing Miss Ford had been dismissed, to be collected by her friend, who was waiting in reception, and hurried out of that place of torment. The interview had been taped and they were playing it back, Gently with a thoughtful pipe in his mouth as he listened, Beamish with narrowed eyes. '"Think what you like . . . I've said all I'm going to say."'

Beamish wound it back and played that part again. 'You got her with the Mondeo, sir. She thought someone might have spotted it – little did she know that she was dropping him in it. And then her lies about what she told him. I'll bet he knew within yards where he could find Thorpe.'

Gently nodded. No problem there.

123

'I'm half beginning to fancy him myself, sir. There's nothing we can prove, but when you put it together ... And the lady doing her nut to keep us off him. Something she knows, I could swear to it, but it's something she's never going to tell us.'

'Yes, the ultimate lie: her pretence of ignorance. Wasn't that the deadliest factor of all?'

'She suspects him, sir.'

Gently puffed.

'Could be something he let drop. The way she's been carrying on from the start, that was a sign. It wasn't just seeing the body.'

'But ... we're short of one feature.'

'Sir?'

'For Hastings, we need a rock-bottom motive. Thorpe strangling the wife is barely enough to fetch such a man on such an errand.'

'A rush of blood, sir?'

'I doubt if Hastings is prone to them.'

'But if all the rest fits, sir?'

'We would still have a weak case. For every circumstance he has an answer, except the testimony of another suspect.'

Beamish made a face. 'So it's back to Norton, sir. No doubt about motive when it comes to him.'

After a pause, Gently slowly nodded. 'But I think we'll extend our enquiries. Any sightings of Hastings to add to Dyball's. Remembering he may have come and gone by Holmeness.'

'We keep him in the frame, sir.'

'We keep him in the frame.'

Beamish sighed, but left it at that.

124

# 9

Gloomily, Gently made his way to the Fisherman's Arms and collected a pint from the bar. Outside on the promenade was a bench-table; he sat himself there and filled a fresh pipe.

A bastard of a case . . .

He sipped and smoked, stared at the sea and ships on the horizon. Festival-goers passed him by; he heard a snatch of conversation in French. Shinglebourne's special week was continuing, with concerts, plays, exhibitions. And the sun. And the sea. While tapes still fluttered outside the old coach . . .

What was he missing?

Somewhere there, in the pattern of it . . .

The dead woman in the flat.

The dead man in the coach.

Dyball. Norton. Hastings. Could there be another, still outside the picture? Were they underrating the disturbed secretary, even her conscientious friend?

Somewhere in the pattern of it . . .

Over and over it was turning in his mind. Something critical, that he was missing. Something that had come to him in his dreams . . .

He drank, smoked, shook his head.

Perhaps it was time for him to retire!

'All ready to arrest me then, are you?'

He looked up to find himself staring at Norton, a Norton who also had a glass in his hand, and who stood regarding him with bitter eyes.

'Don't worry – your hound-dog is with me. In fact, we're becoming quite good friends. When I suggested a trip here this morning, he was quite happy to oblige.'

He gestured to an embarrassed DC Stubbs, who was hovering in the background.

'I didn't think it was out of line, sir,' Stubbs said awkwardly. 'My orders were only to keep an eye on him.'

Gently shrugged. 'So get yourself a drink too.'

'Well, if you say so, sir . . .' He faded into the Fisherman's.

Norton sat himself at the bench-table and took a long, deliberate swallow. He stared at his glass. 'So how much longer?' he asked. 'If you're going to do it, then for Christ's sake get it over.'

Gently blew smoke at him. 'Is that a confession?'

'You know it isn't a sodding confession.'

'So why are you asking me to arrest you?'

Norton snorted and drank more beer. 'I'm still your Number One, aren't I?' he said. 'You're not going to let me out of your sight. And my car, you're hanging on to that, and that bitch of a secretary is swearing I'll clobber her.'

Gently blew more smoke. 'Are you saying you wouldn't?'

'I wouldn't soil my hands.'

'You know Miss Ford well.'

'Too lousy well. Ever since my sister took up with that boss of hers.'

'Whom . . . she worships.'

Norton spat. 'If you're going to blame anyone, blame her. If she'd done the decent thing by Yvonne then none of this need have happened. My sister . . . well, she wasn't promiscuous. I doubt if she had an affair before she married. But she wanted kids, that was her ambition, to have a family of her own.'

'Which – her husband couldn't provide.'

Norton drank. Several couples passed along the promenade, pausing by the rails for a moment to watch a yacht that was heading for the harbour.

Pint in hand, Stubbs emerged from the pub, to lean against the wall at a little distance.

Norton went on staring at his glass. 'She was pregnant. You know that?'

Gently nodded.

126

'She rang me that morning. She had just received confirmation.'

'On the morning – '

'On that morning. She had been round to her GP's. She'd suspected it for quite a while, then made up her mind to have a test and the test was positive. The first thing she did when she got back was to ring me.'

Gently breathed smoke. 'News you had been expecting?'

Norton jerked his shoulder. 'Yes.'

'You were in her confidence?'

'If you like.'

'You knew that Thorpe was the father?'

'Damn it, no!'

'No?'

'I said no.' He shuffled his glass. 'She had a lover. I knew that. We'd talked it over a hundred times, what she should do in her situation and whether I would blame her if she looked elsewhere. I told her no, I wouldn't blame her, and suggested a divorce, but she said that would take too long and she wasn't getting any younger. Then she told me she'd found the right man, a real man, one she wasn't ashamed of. I wanted to know who, but she wouldn't tell me, said I would know later, if it came off.' He slammed the glass on the table. 'And it did come off. I'll never, never forget that phone call. She was so happy, she was out of this world. At last, at last she was going to become a mother . . .'

'But . . . no mention of the father's name.'

He stared at the glass. 'No.'

'And you didn't ask her?'

He shook his head. 'Perhaps, if I'd had the sense to do that . . .'

'It would probably have altered nothing.'

'It . . . just might. If I'd contacted him right away . . .' He took a vicious gulp from the glass. 'But how could I guess – how could anyone have guessed?'

'Guessed that Thorpe would be given the afternoon off?'

'Guessed what he would do when he heard the news.

When they told me, I didn't believe it, it didn't make sense, he must have been bonkers. Why, why did he have to strangle her? She would never have told on him to Hastings, never have threatened him. We're talking of Yvonne, my kid sister, not of some harpy on the make.'

Gently nodded. The news she brought him could scarcely have been unexpected. Her intentions from the start must have been plain to him and previously had not appeared unacceptable. They would have discussed it, made decisions, have anticipated such a conclusion. And yet, when it came ... when the joyous woman sought his embrace with her tidings ...

How, then, had it happened that she had finished up as a corpse on the bed in his flat?

'That call. I can never forget it.'

In her bliss, had some folly been committed?

'It was her dream and it had come true. And then, hours later, she was ... dead.' Norton's knuckles were white as he grasped the glass. 'You're right, I'd have done for that bastard if I'd laid my hands on him. I may have come to my senses since, but not then, not when they told me. What he did to Yvonne I'd have done to him, and sung all the way to the nick.'

'His career might have been jeopardised ...'

'She would never have told on him.'

'I believe her husband was not without suspicions.'

'Sodding Ossie? But he could only have sacked him. And we could probably have found him a place with us.'

'Hastings might also have sued for a divorce.'

Norton scowled. 'So where was the problem? If Thorpe was half the guy that Yvonne thought he was it could have been the best solution for everyone. They could have married, settled down and lived happily ever after. It must have crossed the bastard's mind ... and yet, when it came to the push ...'

'It may have struck him too suddenly.'

'But he couldn't not have expected it.' Norton glared at the glass. 'What the hell *did* happen there?'

128

Gently was silent. Yes, all along that had been the question that lacked an answer, what had happened in that flat to drive Thorpe to such a deed. The news was bringing him trouble certainly, but trouble that could not have been unforeseen – on the contrary. The odds were long that the lady had advised him of her likely condition. Confirmation had been what she brought, not a sudden bolt from the blue. How, then, had it ended as it did, in reckless violence and flight? What was the missing factor in that crime in the Putney flat?

Nothing, no surmise, came to mind. From every view, the crime was inexplicable. While the other, that followed on, had motives that were too transparent.

Except . . .?

Gently drank.

Could the missing factor conceivably be there?

'Bonkers,' Norton said. 'He had to be bonkers, that's the only excuse you can find for him; nothing else fits. And now he's paid for it.' He, too, took a long pull. 'So – who is it to be?'

Gently shrugged.

'Don't think I'm blaming you,' Norton said. 'It all adds up: I was here on the spot and I'm admitting there was a time when I might have done it. But I know what you don't, that it wasn't me who bashed Thorpe, so that leaves someone else. And I don't mean your old tramp.'

Gently shrugged again and struck a match.

'Perhaps you think it's too crazy,' Norton said. 'And perhaps it is. Ossie wouldn't stick his neck out, but that doesn't mean he isn't behind it.'

'Not – behind it?'

Norton spat. 'He's got money and he's got connections. He only had to know where Thorpe was hiding out and his rotten secretary told him that.'

Gently stared, but shook his head.

'Yes, and I'll bet she knows plenty,' Norton said. 'But she'll never talk, that's for certain. She's probably in it as deep as he is.'

Gently blew a ring. 'You think she was his accessory?'

'I wouldn't put it past her.' Norton scowled. 'Don't forget I've known her longer than you have. And that goes for someone else too.'

Two children ran by, pursuing a dog, followed at a distance by their mother. The yacht, a graceful sloop, was putting in a tack to gain ground offshore.

On the beach below a ball game was in progress accompanied by cries and shouts of laughter.

Norton emptied his glass. 'So do I get told – are you looking a little further than me?'

Gently regarded him but said nothing.

Norton slammed the glass down on the table. 'At least I don't get locked up.'

'Your presence here is still required, Mr Norton.'

'Then I can take my hound-dog to lunch?'

'Provided you stay clear of a certain hotel.'

Norton's scowl was bitter, but he said no more, merely jerked to his feet and beckoned to Stubbs. The latter hurriedly tossed back his drink and, after an apologetic glance at Gently, hastened after his charge in the direction of the promenade – opposite to that of the White Hart Hotel . . .

'I can recommend the skate, sir. It was fresh in an hour ago.'

Though it was still early for lunch the White Hart's dining-room was already filling up – Festivallers: a noisy crowd, full of conversation and jest, some circulating from table to table, others gathered in distinct parties. A German clique. A French. Then there were those who shouldered at the bar . . . But, as yet, no sign of the woeful secretary and her friend. Perhaps they were lunching elsewhere, at a venue more private?

Gently collected a drink and chose a small table by one of the windows. Was it credible, that notion of Norton's that Thorpe's murder had been a professional job? The manner was against it. No professional killer would have gone unprovided with a weapon – and that weapon most likely a knife. Violent bludgeoning was out of the picture. But . . . setting that aside? The work of a beginner? Then, a certain credibility obtained. If Hastings indeed had such connections, he also had the means with which to employ them. It was almost possible . . . but not quite. Not if one believed a tenth of Dyball's testimony. The car might have been provided, but the man? His description was not that of a paid killer . . .

Gently sipped and stared at nothing.

Motive also – one always fell back on that.

One way or the other, what could have inspired Hastings to take such action?

He believed Thorpe had murdered his wife, true, but a wife who already was drifting away from him, one whose loss was not so wholly unbearable that he'd risk his all in seeking revenge. Simply, the motive wasn't sufficient. The process of law should have satisfied Hastings. He wasn't a hothead. He wasn't a fool. What would possibly have moved him to a deed so disastrous . . .?

'I can recommend the skate, sir . . .'

'Very well. I'll take it.'

The noise around him was increasing: laughter, raised voices, the high-pitched giggling of some woman. Absently he chewed an item from a dish the waiter had placed on the table, unaware of what it was, and washed it down with a sip from his glass . . .

Motive: Thorpe had had to die, and somewhere in that case was the reason . . . somewhere. And it lay in town – what had happened in Shinglebourne was a mere corollary. At the time it had all seemed straightforward, a crime from the book, no query unanswered; one had merely to lay hands on the culprit and the job was wrapped up, the verdict foregone. Too straightforward . . . was that it? A crime that somehow had been doctored? And one that had left a loose end subsequently to be tidied up at the old coach . . .?

But how? But why? What had he missed?

He frowned at the noisy ones at the next table.

Even now, running over the details, he could light on little that offered any suggestion. Perhaps surprise that, with the Thames so handy, Thorpe hadn't dumped the body and tried to face things out, but there could have been reasons for that, like the possible presence of witnesses. Then again, the lady was pregnant and their association not entirely unknown – no. His flight after the deed was a natural response to what had occurred.

'Your skate, sir ... would you care for some sauce?'

Mechanically he made a start on his fish. It was only then that he saw, at a table across the room, that Miss Ford and her friend had taken their seats.

Had they noticed him? Apparently not. They sat sipping wine and conversing together, Miss Ford with her back to him, her friend with a menu in her hand.

Miss Ford ...

Gently ate.

Back to that day when it happened. A normal day, it had appeared, except for that one rearrangement of routine. The staff had arrived. The boss. Correspondence, conferences, busy phones ... back at Wimbledon an appointment being kept, but no knowledge of that at the office. And so to lunch, which Hastings took at home, where, unsurprisingly, his wife had little appetite – just a plate of soup, Hastings had testified, which the PM was later to confirm. Then, straight after lunch, a call from a client requesting costings for a conference the following morning of a programme which they would deliver ...

Gently paused, his fork in the air. Just a trace of the unusual there? Automatically, he glanced across at Miss Ford, but shook his head and continued eating. Doubtless such arrangements were not uncommon and Thorpe had apparently raised no objection – on the contrary. An afternoon off provided him with a perfect opportunity to consort with his mistress. If, later, the early delivery of the programme had made the arrangement superfluous, that was all in a day's work, wasn't it? Wasn't it . . .? Another glance at the far table.

Either way, Thorpe was at liberty and must have wasted no time in contacting the lady, while she, it appeared, had skipped a hairdressing appointment and hurried to join him at his flat. She had news, such news to tell him – but no, not over the phone. It must wait until she saw him, till she could tell him face to face . . .

Had he guessed what it was? More than likely. By the time she arrived it had begun to sink in. Discussions, plans there may have been, but now the actual event had happened. Suddenly the consequences were upon him: his career at stake, obligations heaped on him. And she, she who was responsible, about to throw herself into his arms . . .

Gently frowned. Was the picture really credible – that Thorpe could have responded in such a way? To accept it, one could only assume that no love had existed between him and the lady . . . that she had been fooled by attentions intended only to secure him her body. For fooled she had been. To her brother she had presented her lover as a sort of dream man.

Well . . . whether or no.

She had finished up dead.

While Thorpe had returned, as expected, to the office, to perform the task allotted to him.

To perform it . . . why? Where was the necessity? Once the staff had left there had been nothing to keep him. When the door had finally closed on them he could have robbed the safe and made off.

Gently drank, ate his last few chips, stared for some moments at the empty plate.

Almost, one could think, Thorpe was innocent of any knowledge of what was waiting back there in the flat. Some hours had been required to complete the costing, hours that might have been vital to his escape – Hastings, for example, when he missed his wife, might have started enquiries that could have proved fatal . . .

133

Had he been in shock? Working mechanically? Unable at once to plan what his next move should be?

Possible, perhaps, but . . .

In the end he had acted promptly and intelligently enough.

'A sweet, sir?'

'A sweet . . . the gateau.'

'And coffee after . . .?'

'I'll take it in the lounge.'

The waiter whisked away his plate and moments later returned with the sweet. Absently Gently tackled it.

Yes – at the end of the day. With the job done and the cash in his pocket, Thorpe had hastened back to pack a bag and scarper, and the presence of that pitiful corpse hadn't prevented an intelligent decision. Town wouldn't do. The search would begin there. Also, taking lodgings was a dangerous step. It called for a location they wouldn't connect with him, a refuge that was off the road. And such a place he knew of: in that desperate moment a memory from his childhood flashed into his brain – Suffolk, the old coach, set aside from a town where he was a stranger. And, if the worst came to the worst, handy for a ferry port across to Holland . . .

The complete picture.

And he had accepted it.

With every query along the line.

Savagely Gently emptied his plate and threw back the dregs from his glass.

And now. Now?

He stared at nothing. Something had suddenly focused in his mind, a point, a small point, but the one that had troubled his sleep the previous night. The hairdresser . . . what had she said? That she'd been surprised by the broken appointment . . . that always, on previous occasions, Mrs Hastings had rung her when she couldn't keep one. Against all the other facts a trifle, perhaps to be attributed to the latter's state of mind . . . Or perhaps . . .?

Now his stare reached across the room.

The two ladies had risen, were making their way towards the lounge.


'I've nothing to say to you. Nothing.'

The lounge, conveniently, was almost empty, just one other table occupied and that at the further end of the room. There sat four garrulous Festivallers, intent on no one but themselves. Coffee had been served to Miss Ford and her friend; the former had stiffened when her eye caught Gently.

'You have no right to keep harassing me – everything I know I've already told you. And if you don't take the matter from there, then you're not the man you're given out to be.'

'Hush, Chrissie,' Madge murmured. 'There's no need to create a scene.'

'I don't care, it isn't fair.'

'He's only doing his job.'

'Then he can leave us alone.'

Silently Gently took a seat at their table and filled, but didn't light, his pipe. The waiter fetched his coffee and his bill, and he paid it. The two ladies watched with resentful eyes.

'So what's it about – why are you plaguing us?'

Gently sipped. 'A small matter you can help me with.'

'But for heaven's sake, what?'

'I'd like you to think back to the day all this started, in town.'

'What happened then . . .'

He nodded.

'But we went over all that at the time!'

'I seem to have forgotten the name of that company – the one who required a costing from you.'

'Their – name?' Her eyes were suddenly still.

'It was Windows, wasn't it?' Miss Simpson said. 'I seem to remember . . .'

'All right, Madge. But why is he asking about it now?'

135

Gently shrugged. 'You would have taken the call?'

'Yes, that's my job. And I informed Mr Hastings.'

'With the time when you could expect delivery of the programme?'

'When – no. They couldn't give a definite time.'

'Just . . . at their earliest.'

'If you like.'

'Which in fact was quite promptly, as it turned out.'

'But we couldn't have known – '

'Are you sure, Miss Ford?'

'Yes. Why else would we have arranged for Thorpe – '

'Arranged for him to spend that evening at the office?'

'Yes – he sometimes did that. It was nothing new.'

Gently shook his head. 'At whose suggestion was it?'

'At Ossie's – mine. I suggested it to him . . .'

'It was the idea of Mr Hastings?'

'No!'

'But I think it would have been, Miss Ford.'

'No. No!'

It had to happen. The tears overflowed and she was stifling sobs. Madge Simpson's arm crept round her shoulders, but Miss Ford thrust it aside. With an effort she overcame the sobs, brushed away the tears and fixed her blue-hazel eyes on Gently's. 'You're trying to trap me, aren't you?'

Gently watched her but said nothing.

'Yes, you've got some stupid idea in your head and you're trying to make me say things that will back it up.'

'What stupid idea, Miss Ford?'

'I don't know. About Ossie. That brother-in-law of his has got at you and now you're trying to shift the blame. But it won't work. There was nothing strange about what happened in the office. Those figures were needed, we couldn't take the risk, and we took the usual course of action. And that's all.'

Slowly Gently nodded. 'So . . . Thorpe was released for the afternoon.'

'Yes – and you can't blame us. We didn't know what he was going to do.'

'But, when you did know?'

'How do you mean?'

'Did nothing strange strike you then, Miss Ford? That afterwards Thorpe should return to the office and spend several hours completing those costings?'

'But – '

'Yes?'

A flicker of fear.

'Well?'

'How – how should I know how his mind worked? He may have thought that if he acted the innocent there was a chance of him getting away with it.'

'But with the body lying in his flat?'

'Perhaps he imagined he could get rid of it.'

'And with such thoughts he still completed his job?'

'Yes – why not?'

Gently shook his head. 'The picture we're looking at is different, Miss Ford. It's the picture of a man devoid of such knowledge. A man as yet with nothing on his mind but the job he has undertaken to perform.'

'But you're guessing – '

'I'm looking at the facts. Thorpe arrived at the office with an unburdened mind.'

'Then – then it happened later. When he got back.'

Gently paused, but shook his head again. The medical evidence had shown otherwise. It had been several hours earlier when Yvonne Hastings met her end.

'He robbed the safe – you can't get away from it.'

'I think he returned to do that.'

'But why, when he was on the spot?'

'Because then, he wouldn't know that he needed to.'

'You're guessing – guessing!'

'Looking at facts. Facts represented by a sheet of figures.'

'It's crazy, all of it – crazy, I tell you. You're just trying to shift blame from Norton . . .'

137

'Easy, Chrissie, easy.' Madge Simpson was trying to hug her again. 'There are people here – they're watching us. Do try to keep your voice down.'

Another party had entered the lounge and were glancing curiously in their direction. Then they exchanged a word among themselves and proceeded to a table at a little distance.

'We do have to live here, you know.'

'But you've heard him – and it isn't fair.'

'We know that, but he doesn't.'

'He does. He does. And he's trying to trap me.'

'Still . . .'

The tears were back.

Madge Simpson supplied her friend with a handkerchief. Then she drank some cold coffee and turned her dark eyes on Gently. 'Ask me some questions! I was there. If there's anything you want to know . . .'

Gently lit his pipe, adjusting it carefully and blowing smoke away from the two women. He said: 'That afternoon. Did everything continue as usual at the office?'

'Of course it did. What do you mean?'

'The usual staff – they were all there?'

'As far as I know . . .'

'The boss among them?'

'Mr Hastings never left the office.' Her eyes were sharp. 'Ask anyone. It was the same as any other afternoon.'

'He arrived as usual?'

'If anything, earlier. He was parking as I returned from lunch – I remember remarking on it to someone. And later, I delivered some files to his office.'

'Everything as usual . . .'

'Yes. Everything.'

Gently nodded. 'Thank you, Miss Simpson.'

'Oh!' She slammed down her cup and jerked to her feet. 'Come on, Chrissie. We've had enough of this. Let him pester other people with his clever questions.'

'But he's trying to say . . .'

'Never mind. He's had quite a long enough session with

138

us.' And she hauled Miss Ford from her chair and towed her off through the swing doors.

But Gently sat a while longer. In fact, till he'd finished his pipe.

# 10

Gulls were squealing along the tide line and a light offshore breeze fluttered the ribbons. A couple were strolling along the marrams, pausing every now and then to gaze out to sea.

Instead of returning direct to the office, Gently had made his way once more to the old coach, stood now by the doorway, hands clasped behind him, letting his eyes wander over the prospect.

The hut. The distant town. The roofs and upper windows of the White Hart Hotel . . . did a curtain stir there?

Without question, if an observer had been at one of those windows . . .

If . . .

He made a face and turned his stare back to the sea.

Nothing could be expected from that direction.

Dyball was all. Dyball . . .

He leaned against the door, his gaze bitter. Could he really have been such a fool? The pattern had been there from the beginning, yet only now had he begun to glimpse it. What happened here had been only a corollary – yes, he had understood that. But its intent, that had remained obscure, its true purpose, that which provoked it. It had stayed at revenge, or at the outside robbery – with queries perhaps, but until now . . .

And if he hadn't been fooled, had spotted it earlier?

He stared and stared at the apron of sea.

Then, even then, the odds were that he couldn't have prevented what happened here. There were few angles to have offered progress and only contact with Thorpe could have supplied them. An appeal? He would probably have ignored it, seen it merely as a trap to get him into their hands . . .

Savagely Gently thrust open the door of the coach and scowled at the dank interior, at the bed, at the dishevelled sacks, one with stains still showing on it.

He wasn't responsible and yet . . .

He slammed the door violently. He couldn't help it. Thorpe's death was weighing on him. But for his blindness it might not have happened.

And now – now?

The banging of the door had sent a hen pheasant skirling from some brambles and attracted the attention of the two strollers, who paused to stare across at him. He glared back and saw the man shrug; then they continued on their way . . .

He drew a deep breath, felt for his pipe and set off in the direction of the town.

Perhaps it *was* time for him to retire . . .

Hands in pockets, he strode by the White Hart, shouldering past a group of emerging Festivallers.


'What shall we do about Dyball, sir? Either we charge him, or we'll have to let him go.'

That wasn't the only problem he found awaiting him at the office. A disgruntled Stubbs had reported in – Norton had contrived to give him the slip. At lunch he had gone to the toilet, but had failed to reappear and, when Stubbs had gone to investigate, all he had found was an open window. Did it matter . . .? Probably not. A mere gesture on the part of the estate agent. Stubbs had been brought back to cover the inn at Thwaite and meanwhile Norton's car remained impounded at the police station . . .

'Dyball did pinch the money, sir, to put it no higher. And we can do him for not reporting the body.'

Gently shrugged. 'Is there a lodging here that you sometimes make use of in cases like this?'

'Well, yes, there is . . .'

'So discharge him with a warning and a man to keep an eye on him.'

Beamish looked blank. 'If you say so, sir.'

'First of all, we need Dyball as a witness.'

It was done. A not unhappy Dyball was escorted to a room in a local hostel, primed as to what was expected of him and left in the charge of a DC.

'But can we really depend on what he tells us, sir?'

Or, more to the point, would a jury believe him? Gently puffed at his pipe grimly. As the case stood, no doubt about the answer. Circumstance and Dyball were not enough; what they needed was something more damning: for example, a supporting witness . . . like one who might have watched from a certain window. But no hope there. And so?

He laid down his pipe. 'Hand me that file.'

In it was the number of Hastings's office. He rang and was answered by the voice of a woman.

'May I please speak to Mr Hastings?'

'I'm sorry, sir, but Mr Hastings has just left. Can I take a message?'

'Be kind enough to ask him to ring this number when he returns. Will he be gone long?'

'I'm afraid I couldn't say, sir. May I have your name?'

Gently gave it.

'I will pass your message on, sir, as soon as he returns.'

'And please stress that it is important.'

He hung up.

Beamish was watching him. 'Putting a bit of pressure on him, sir?'

Gently shrugged. 'One way or another! We need Hastings back in this office.'

'But if he won't play, sir?'

'Then he'll be fetched. Oswald Hastings has questions to answer. And if he refuses an ID parade then we shall want to know the reason why.'

'You – you'd really go through with that, sir?'

'At this stage, pressure is all we've got.'

Beamish didn't exactly shake his head, but he looked away in studied silence.

'There are . . . reasons.'

Only at that moment he wasn't in the mood to discuss them. Soon enough he would have to admit that, from the beginning, he'd been taken in. Enough, meanwhile, that Hastings was in the frame, however questionable his apparent motive; the rest could come later, would perhaps appear as the action developed . . .

That: it was the husband. Not the lover.

That: the latter had been set up.

And that, he had had to be silenced.

That was the true picture in the frame!

'I suppose you're right, sir, and we'll have to fetch him in. But I can't see it getting us very far.'

Morosely Gently relit his pipe and scowled at the sheets in the file in front of him. They direly needed a supporting witness, one whose testimony could not be questioned. At this end the search had been thorough and there was small chance of one turning up now, but at the other . . .? He drilled smoke. There, a fortnight had passed since the crime was committed, too long a period to expect results in tracing the movements of a certain person . . . Yet, if the right questions were asked?

He picked up the phone again and stabbed a familiar number. 'Dutt?'

'Sir? I was going to ring you. I checked on that posh Mondeo of Hastings's . . .'

And no, on the date of the crime at Shinglebourne it hadn't been in the garage for service or repair.

'So listen, Dutt.'

In few words he gave the cockney inspector his instructions: a trace on the movements of Oswald Hastings on the day his wife had died, beginning at lunch-time at the villa in Wimbledon, through to the evening of that day. His departures, his returns, any sightings at the critical scene, any remembered incidents, the most trivial to be recorded.

'I'll put a couple of the boys on it, sir. Do you reckon we've rumbled something?'

144

'Take it that we have, Dutt.'

'Yes, sir . . . I've always wondered about that geezer. He could have pulled it, him, both the job here and the one out there.'

'So use your initiative, Dutt.'

'You bet sir! If the goods are there we'll have them.'

He hung up and struck a fresh light.

Now Beamish really was staring! 'Are you seriously thinking, sir . . .?'

After a pause, Gently nodded his head.

'It wasn't Thorpe?'

'He was set up. By a very clever man.'

'But Holy Moses . . .!'

'A man who, till now, hasn't offered us a handle.'

'We can't pull him?'

'Perhaps we'll decide that when we've got him sitting in that chair.'

'But . . . stone the crows!' Beamish looked shaken. He stared at Gently, at the chair. 'And all this time, sir . . .?'

'No.' Unwillingly, Gently shook his head. 'Mistakes get made sometimes, even by people who should know better. And this was one of those times.'

'Well, I don't know, sir!'

Gently breathed smoke. 'What we need now is a ring on that phone.'


But the afternoon wore on and the phone stayed resolutely silent. Meanwhile, other business claimed Beamish and Gently was left to keep his vigil alone. He smoked, drank the coffee they brought him and stared at the traffic in the street. Out there, overcast was drifting in from the sea and a few drops of rain were beginning to fall.

A wet night in prospect . . . such a night as had obscured that occasion in town, when a late-working accountant had hastened back to his flat from the office. Till then, he hadn't guessed that his absence had been engineered and that his work could as well have been done in the afternoon. In perfect unconcern he had crossed the paved approach and hurried down the steps to the sheltered area below . . .

Gently scowled at the passing cars. And the body – how long had it been there? At a guess, the dumping would have been delayed until the last possible moment. Darkness and an absence of witnesses was essential, a degree of risk had to be accepted – quite possibly, Hastings had first driven past the office to check that a light was still showing in the window. It was and he'd made his play, backing in to hoist the body down those steps, leaving it there behind the tubs of plants, in the obscurity, sheltered from the rain. And so back to Wimbledon to advise the police that his wife was missing . . .

Why had he, Gently, been so blind? The PM report might have warned him. The pregnancy, the contents of the stomach, almost the moment of her death had been written there. Now, the manner of it was only too plain. At that fatal lunch she couldn't hide her news from him. Her dream had come true, she had to tell it, to a husband whose suspicions had already been roused . . . was it barely possible she could have believed he would accept her state as an act of his own? Too soon she learned different. His rage was instant, he accused her of being a lying whore, all her excuses were thrust aside and the name of her lover thrown at her – while she, on her side, accused him of trapping her in a sterile marriage. And so it had ended, with her lifeless body sliding from his hands to the floor . . . and Hastings left in a situation calling for swift, unhesitating action.

Gently knocked out his pipe savagely, mechanically filled and lit it again.

Had Hastings known at the time of that requirement by one of his clients?

His lying secretary had denied it, which rather indicated the reverse. But either way, it had come to hand and Hastings had wasted no time in making use of it. The lover had to be set up. He had to be provided with opportunity.

And while the free afternoon offered him that, it also secured his absence from the flat later. A perfect ploy. In utter innocence Thorpe had walked into the snare set for him. He may even, as they had supposed, tried to ring his mistress, on the chance of setting up a rendezvous. But the phone had rung in a silent house and he had spent the afternoon alone . . . knowing nothing, guessing nothing, till he reached the sanctuary at the foot of the steps.

Gently paused to study that picture, the lover confronted with the body of his mistress. Shock, horror, disbelief . . . and then a deadly realisation . . .

The events of that day flashed through his mind and at once they made terrible sense. He had been trapped. The guilt had been cast on him and nothing he could tell would receive credit for a moment. Worse, if they discovered what she had been suspecting – a motive there, they would surely argue. So . . . so . . .?'

In tears and terror he'd lugged the body into the flat and laid it reverently out on the bed where, later, the police were to find it. No option, he must run. Perhaps, one day, the real truth would come out. But now . . . now . . .? He stuffed clothes in a case, tried somehow to plan for the nightmare ahead. Money . . . he knew where to find that . . . but a place of refuge, where none would seek him . . .? Lodgings, no – in town, no – somewhere outside, some-where . . . And into his mind had darted the image of the old coach. There – there! The perfect sanctuary. A hide-out in country where none knew him, yes, yes! A place of safety, where he could stay and watch events . . .

And so he had taken his tearful farewell and hastened into the dark night . . . ignorant, alas, of a circumstance that could turn that sanctuary into a death-trap. And . . . did.

The secretary had shopped him.

For Hastings, an arrest had seemed too perilous. Fear, not revenge had been the motive that sent Oswald Hastings to that spot . . .

Gently bit hard on the stem of his pipe.

Because, for the second time, hadn't Hastings brought it off? Leaving only circumstance and suspicion on which to build a case, if a case they should bring?

A smudged dab and the testimony of a liar was the only hard substance they had to offer, neither of which would cause much grief to the sort of counsel that Hastings could afford.

They could bring pressure, real pressure, but was there the smallest chance they could get him to confess?

Gently pictured the bold brown eyes, the stubborn jaw, the calculated voice.

Perhaps . . . perhaps . . .

But they must bring him here, with consent or without, to undergo all they could throw at him: Dyball, dabs check, hours of questioning, the knowledge that the pattern of his crimes was understood . . . would it be enough?

He glared at the telephone, which so resolutely refused to ring.

Probably not. But failing some lucky break, that was the only course of action left to them . . .

'Sir, we've picked up Norton again. He was trying to have another go at the secretary. I told him flat out that unless he played ball we would shove him in a cell and had him escorted back to Thwaite.'

Gently merely shrugged.

'No doubt in his mind, sir. He swore that Hastings was the man we should go for and that she knows it, too. Do you reckon we should give her another innings?'

'It may come to that.'

'But he hasn't rung, sir?'

'Not yet.'

'Do you think he's going to?'

Gently glanced at his watch. It was after five – time, surely, for Hastings to have returned to his office?

He reached for the phone. 'May I speak to Mr Hastings?'

'Oh, it's you, sir. No, I'm afraid not.'

'He hasn't come in?'

'Not yet, sir, though he may do before he goes home.'

'Didn't he say where he was going?'

'Someone rang him and he just said he would have to go out. If it's really important I'll leave a note on his desk and a message on his answering machine at home. Do you wish me to do that?'

'I wish to speak to him at the earliest.'

'I'll make sure he gets the message, sir. Though he often dines out and may not be in till quite late.'

'And you haven't the smallest idea of who rang him?'

'Sorry, sir. He took the call himself.'

'At what time would that be?'

'As I remember, somewhere between half past two and three.'

Gently hung up, frowning. Another report from the worshipful Miss Ford? The timing matched. It would have been about two thirty when she was steered from the lounge of the White Hart . . .

'You think he's dodging us, sir?'

'It's possible. It may come to us having to have him picked up.'

'Perhaps we'd better give him a chance, sir.'

But Hastings wasn't the sort to whom one gave chances.

Slowly, irritably, Gently scraped out his pipe and refilled it for the umpteenth time. Sooner or later . . . so why not sooner? In his mind, was there still any shred of doubt? Once there'd been none where some should have existed, but not here, not here. Each time he went over the picture afresh it gathered strength and stood out plainer . . . So why wait, why retain the kid gloves, when a brief call on the phone . . .? Caution perhaps, only caution . . . and the knowledge that he was up against a formidable opponent.

'Maybe it is time again to talk to Miss Ford.'

'I was waiting for you to say that, sir. Norton reckons she's in it up to her neck and we only have to lean on her.'

'Something she has to know.'

'Right, sir. It was her who gave Hastings the word. And then she waited to give him his chance before she let on to us.'

'Which suggests something else.'

'She was in from the start . . .'

'At least that she had her suspicions.'

Beamish nodded eagerly. 'So I fetch her in, sir?'

But the ringing of the phone interrupted them.


'A spot of info, old man. What's the weather like with you?'

The call was coming from the Yard and the caller was Commander Pagram. Gently's immediate superior, he rarely came directly to the point; Gently eased back in his chair and stared at the rain, which now was falling steadily.

'It's teeming down here and if you don't have a brolly you're stuck. Poor old Dutt looked quite sodden when he came in a few moments ago.'

'Dutt . . .?'

'He'd been over to Putney doing your errands, old lad, but he had to chase off again, following a lead, and asked me to pass on a message. The Thorpe affair, you know. If we should still be calling it that.'

'He has a lead?'

'That's the impression.'

It was no use hurrying Pagram.

'A couple called Taylor,' Pagram said. 'Retired people. He used to work in someone's bank. You wouldn't have come across them. They have a married daughter, who lives in Florida. And that's the point. She lives in Florida. They pay her a visit there every now and then.'

Gently grunted. In the end they would get there.

'The other point is where they reside,' Pagram said. 'Which is number twenty-four Riverside. Does that grab your interest, old lad?'

'Number twenty-four . . .'

'Just across the road, in fact, Dutt says, bang opposite. From their sitting-room window you look straight over to the steps of a certain basement flat. And now the points add together. The Taylors were booked on a night flight to

150

Miami. They were all packed and ready, and waiting for a taxi to Heathrow. Isn't it odd, old fellow, how coincidences happen in this game?'

'On . . . that same night?'

'Bingo.'

'And they saw something?'

'We're coming to it. Like I say, they were packed and ready, and waiting for a taxi due at ten p.m. So when they heard a car pull up outside they tweaked the curtains and took a shufti.'

'But – it wasn't the taxi.'

'It wasn't the taxi.'

'Could they describe it?'

'Patience, old man. What they saw was a largish vehicle backed into the parking opposite. It was wet, a dark night and the street lighting in Riverside is minimal, and the car wasn't their taxi, so they dropped the curtain again.'

'And that's it?'

'Patience, I said. It get's better as it goes on. Only moments later they heard an engine again and were back at the window. The same car driving away and, strangely, without switching on its lights, but just then their taxi turned into Riverside and its lights lit up the other one. A red car. Largish. A Mondeo, the taxi-driver told them. A sod he knew. A customer . . . why was the bugger driving without his lights?'

'Hastings . . .'

'No name was mentioned, which is why Dutt is still braving the downpour. And from what he tells me, this little news item doesn't take you entirely by surprise?'

Gently was silent.

'Sad,' Pagram said. 'Sad. Then the surprise is entirely on my side. But doubtless the events in Festival country have offered an insight denied to yours truly. Am I on the mark?'

'You are on the mark.'

'So then, to business,' Pagram said. 'Do I shunt our careless driver to Shinglebourne, or would you sooner we kept him here?'

151

Gently hesitated. No need for caution now. 'Arrest him,' he said, 'and fetch him to me.'

'How did I guess?' Pagram said. 'Those are the orders I've already given. I should go out and have a drink, old man, because you're in for a busy evening. Oh, and George –'

'Yes?'

'Don't forget your raincoat. That idiot Dutt has left his at home.'


The advice was sound. Outside the rain was pelting down in deserted streets, and every now and then a grumble of thunder could be heard. Swathes rose from the wheels of passing cars, black cloud was tumbling in from the sea . . . for the moment, summer was over. And the weather seemed to suit the occasion.

'Nothing to do but wait now, sir.'

Pagram's other advice they had also taken. At the pub that was nearest to the police station they sat with pints and plates of sandwiches in front of them. A dreary place: only two other customers had braved the conditions, while the landlord, after serving them, had retired from the bar.

'Tomorrow, we will need an ID parade.'

'Shouldn't be too difficult sir.'

'We'll take his dabs tonight.'

'A pity it's such a poor one on the poker, sir.'

Poor: but it would have to do.

'Do you reckon it's likely we'll get a cough, sir?'

Gently shrugged and drank his beer. No way was Hastings going to make it easy for them. The likelihood was he would close up tight and utter not a word till he'd spoken to a lawyer.

'Tonight, we'll keep it short and leave him to sweat on it in his cell. And tomorrow we won't be in any hurry. We'll wait till after the ID parade.'

'Getting him worried, sir.'

'We can but try.'

Beamish reached for a sandwich and began to chew it. 'It might work, sir.' But he didn't sound hopeful. 'He's a rum bloke, that one, however you look at him.'

A little later, the pub was invaded by a troop of noisy teenagers.

Back in the office the phone was ringing and Gently hastened to snatch it up.

'Sir?'

'Dutt?'

'I've just got back in, sir – I thought I'd try to have a word with you. That taxi-driver, I've traced him, he works for a firm right there in Fulham and he knows Hastings well, swears it was him he met driving away that night.'

'You took his statement?'

'You bet, sir. And I've got one from the Taylors. So there's no doubt about it now – it was Hastings there, dumping the body.'

'Has he been picked up yet?'

'Don't know that he has, sir, but I've only just got in. They've got men watching his house and his office, but if he's out on the town it could be a while yet.'

'Thank you, Dutt. You'd better get along home.'

'Yes, sir – I could use a change of my things.'

Slowly, Gently hung up.

'Was that to tell us they've got him, sir?' Beamish said.

Gently shook his head. 'Perhaps something more vital.'

He related Dutt's message to the local man.

'So he's really set up.'

'For the murder of his wife.'

'But that led on to what he did here, sir. There can't be much doubt about it now, whether he keeps his trap shut or not.'

'We're still dealing with a difficult man.'

'But I mean, sir!' And Beamish's expression suggested that was a trifle.

Still the rain was pelting outside and darkness had fallen unusually early. Gently smoked pipes, drank coffee, went to stare at the rain-swept street. For Beamish the waiting was less onerous since he had routine matters to engage his attention: a drunk was brought in, a street-girl, a youth who had glassed a rival outside a club. Ten o'clock, pushing on eleven ... was that call never going to come through?

'Perhaps it will be tomorrow now, sir.'

But if so, they would surely have been advised? His fingers were itching to pick up the phone when, at the stroke of eleven, ring it did.

'For you, sir . . .'

It was Pagram. 'Sorry to keep you up, old fellow.'

'You have arrested him?'

'Alack and goddamn, I'm afraid we were too late on the job.'

'You mean . . .?'

'Just so. We've been having a chat with a neighbour at Wimbledon. Mid-afternoon was the time to have been there, so the lady tells us – name of Wainwright.'

'Mid-afternoon . . .'

'Didn't he have a phone call? It must have been straight after that. Seems he drove home, garaged the Mondeo and took off again in a spritely Fiesta. You wouldn't have the number?'

'Then we've lost him?'

'Look on the bright side, old lad. He isn't a Lord Lucan, just a wandering fugitive, and the word's out to every point of exit. By morning it's likely he'll be in our hands and on his way to our celebrated sleuth.'

'He is not without means.'

'Oh, phoo!'

'He could have been planning this before today.'

'My dear old pessimist, cheer up. This business seems to be getting you down. But the hounds are out, the game is up and now you've a chance of a night's sleep, so count your blessings and leave it with us. Believe me, no stone will be left unturned.'

The phone went dead.

For a long while, Gently sat with it in his hand.

154

# 11

'Have you seen the paper, sir?'

The next day was the last one of the Festival, grey, overcast after the rain, the wet streets laced with puddles.

Gently had slept late; there had seemed little point in hastening to the office. As gloomy as the weather, he had taken his bath, dressed and gone down to breakfast. The papers had lain on the table, carefully arranged there by Mrs Jarvis, and it wasn't until he had eaten and lit his first pipe that he'd bothered to turn them over. Even then he had almost missed it: a brief paragraph in the stop-press. It read: 'Abandoned car at Beachy Head. Search by police and coastguards in progress. Car found parked within yards of cliff edge. Door on driver's side left open.'

'What do you reckon, sir – could it be him?'

'Has there been any message?'

'Not as yet, sir.'

'Beachy Head is notorious for suicides.'

'It's still a bit of a coincidence, sir.'

'True, but we'd better not jump to conclusions. Especially when we're dealing with Oswald Hastings.'

'Well, if you say so, sir. But I couldn't help wondering, when I saw that.'

A copy of the paper lay on the desk and Gently scanned the paragraph afresh. Few words, but a typical picture of such tragic events as had occurred there before. The mighty cliffs, the tiny car perched at the rim of that dizzying drop, the lonely driver sitting staring at the void – then the moment when the door was thrust open. Did it fit Hastings? He shook his head. The character of the man argued against it. Hastings was a planner, he would fight his corner. Jumping off cliffs was not in his nature . . .

'Just an idea, sir, but that secretary. Do you reckon he might get in touch with her?'

Gently shrugged. 'I think it unlikely. At least, until he's satisfied he's safely away.'

'We could bug the phone over there, sir.'

'There can be no harm in it.'

'Right, sir. I'll do that straight away. And if there's anything else . . .'

Gently merely sighed and after a pause Beamish hastened from the office.

Time . . . time had been the factor. How long had Hastings had before the net was spread? Several hours it was certain, sufficient time for a man like him. Heathrow . . . Gatwick . . . even Luton. Perhaps, in one of their car-parks, the Fiesta was nestling, commonplace and unremarked. Then a switch of flights at Paris, Rome . . . He would have arranged funding long since. The world was his oyster. East or west. New York . . . Singapore . . . Rio . . .

He might not be Lord Lucan, but his disappearance could be equally effectual, while a faked passport would be a trifle to a man like Oswald Hastings . . .

Happily, the affair was in the hands of Pagram, who was unlikely to miss considerations of this sort, and one of whose first moves would have been to alert Interpol. The world might be Hastings's oyster, but now it would be primed with snares to take him. Would they succeed? Gently shrugged! The odds were probably less than even. Always, Hastings had been a move ahead. Too much to hope for a false step this time . . .

He ground his teeth and stared at vacancy.

Why hadn't he weighed up this man earlier?

The phone went: Dutt. 'Did you see that bit in the paper, sir . . .?'

'Which bit?'

'About the car they found at Beachy Head, sir.'

'So what about it?'

'It was the one, sir. We got the details from the DVLA.'

'That car was Hastings' . . .?'

156

'Well, his wife's. The one he was seen driving off in from Wimbledon. Right on the edge of the cliff they found it and he hadn't even put the brake on. We don't think there can be much doubt, sir, and they're searching for the body now.'

But would they find it? 'Did he leave a note?'

'Haven't heard of one, sir.'

'Is Pagram available?'

'He's on the phone to them.'

'Ask him to ring me when he's through.'

He lit a pipe and crushed the match in the ashtray.

Ten minutes elapsed before Pagram rang.

'Old man . . .?'

'Let's have it. Have they found the body?'

'You're so impatient, dear old chap!'

'Well – have they?'

'In so many words, and between you and me, no. Or not yet.'

'And do they still expect to?'

'Why not, laddie? These things take a little time. The bodies down there don't just hang about, they tend to romp around in the currents and the tides.'

'And they've been searching how long?'

'Since first light.'

'But still no sign?'

'Oh dear! Do I detect the sound of naughty thoughts coming over this line, old lad?'

'You certainly do.'

'But there's no cause. I've had a longish talk with the locals. A classic case is what they tell me, the sort they are handling all the time. Jumping from Beachy is all the rage, it beats the Severn Bridge hollow. A couple of corpses on your mind and Beachy is the place to head for.'

'Unless your name is Oswald Hastings.'

'Old man, you're giving him too much credit.'

'I wish I were.'

'Then hear me tell you.'

Gently bit on a pipe gone cold.

'Listen,' Pagram said, 'my dear fellow. You're letting this villain get you down. He fooled us once, but not for long, and he still remains a human being. He makes mistakes and bashing Thorpe was one. After that his time was limited. A double life sentence was facing him and he had a devil like you on his tail. What was left for him? A trip to Beachy. And a trip to Beachy is what he made. Superhuman he wasn't and, on the bright side, he's saved us a deal of trouble and expense.'

'All we have is the car . . .'

He heard Pagram sigh. 'Then, for your sake, I hope we find the body. But fear not, if it doesn't turn up I'll keep the hounds on for a spell. And George.'

'Well?'

'The sun is out here. With any luck, you'll be having it your way.'

He was right. Outside on the street a glimmer of radiance was showing through, and slowly strengthening. After all, the last day of the Festival was to be a fine one . . .

Beamish came in. 'I've done what we said, sir.'

Did that, or anything else, matter any more?

BEACHY HEAD CLAIMS MURDER SUSPECT
*Festival Killer Escapes Justice*

Deliberately he had refrained from ringing the Yard, or even from showing his face at the police station. It was out of his hands now, the tidying up belonged to Pagram and two days later the latter had seen fit to release information to the press. No body . . . but that was quite usual when a search had been delayed. While the two days represented the period during which a wider alert had been maintained . . .

The Festival had packed up and the visitors had gone, including Miss Ford and her friend, and Norton. Dyball, too, had been dismissed, after some hesitation on the part of Beamish. But Gently had prevailed. So little point! And meanwhile the down-and-out had succeeded in signing on . . . Vanished, also, were the striped ribbons that had fluttered outside the old coach . . .

'My dear, why are you so sad? Aha, it is time that I come home!'

Gabrielle had arrived back from Rouen on the Sunday, full of amusing news to tell. But clearly dear George was not in the mood . . . 'You do not like what happens to this man?'

How could he explain? It could be that, once more, he was nursing a mistake about Oswald Hastings . . .

'My dear, it is for the best. Too much to heart you take these things. I tell you, yes? But now I am home and it is time to put them away. So, shall we take our stroll?'

And their stroll they took, through the acres of heather.

In the evening Reymerston and his wife called in, and the talk was all of Gabrielle's trip.

'This is better, my dear. You are looking more cheerful.'

He shrugged and smoked his last pipe.

Perhaps . . . somewhere? He put it out of his mind!

One mistake, he didn't mean to make.